Black Ink Publications Presents
Bad Cop 3
A Novel By
Sa'id Salaam

I0640213

Email: saidmsalaam@gmail.com and/or blackinkpublications1@gmail.com

Facebook: Free Sa'id Salaam

Cover design and layout by: Sunny Giovonni

Edited by: Tisha Andrews

Chapter 1

*T*his saga began with me at my own funeral. So, it obviously ends with my death. A lot happens between my life and death. Some good, some bad. Being a cop was the best, until it became the worse...

"How can I help you?" Megan asked with a smile even though she wanted to scream. She became a police officer to help people but the help desk wasn't quite what she had in mind. People came to the precinct with some of the dumbest shit in the world. By the end of her first year she had heard it all. Or so she thought.

"Yeah, my brother stole my dope!" a man fumed and dug into his bag to produce his proof. "I had two and a half ounces of coke and look! What does that say?"

"Looks like it's about an ounce shy?" she agreed checking out the drugs on the digital scale he brought along with him. Even this wasn't a first in this precinct. "Sarge, we got another one!"

"Send him on back," the duty sergeant called. Megan directed him to the rear where they locked his dumb ass up.

"I can't... " she decided and stood. After a year riding a desk while others got the glory was all she could stand. She marched upstairs to the captain's office and knocked on the door.

"Shit!" he fussed and clicked from the porn site he was perusing. "Come in!"

"Captain Milner, I joined the force to fight crime! Not be a secretary!" she demanded with a hand on her hip. The captain cocked his head curiously but didn't speak. "So I um, um?"

"Want to be reassigned? Patrol?" he asked to help this along so he could get back to *Ghetto Booty*.

"Yes!" she said snapping to attention. The captain pursed his lips and looked her up and down. He noticed she wore her uniform modestly loose while most female officers wore theirs skin tight like jeans. She was always on time and her paperwork was always complete. She was definitely her father's daughter.

"No! Now close the door on your way out!" he fussed. Rohan was one of his partners and friends. No way was he putting his daughter in harm's way. The streets of Harlem were extremely dangerous and he didn't want her to end up dead like her dad.

"But I'm tired of desk duty!" she pouted and stomped her foot. The captain furrowed his brow to reiterate his command to leave. "Oh, OK. Thanks for nothing captain!"

"Sheesh," he sighed and clicked back to the booty. Out came his penis so he could squeeze one before lunch. Megan went back to her desk for another day shoveling shit.

"Good afternoon. How can I help you?" she asked with the gloom of realizing she was stuck desk duty. Knowing she was just a secretary in a cop costume almost made her cry.

"Yeah, my husband done fucked around and fucked my sister!" a lady fumed with hands on hips. "I let this little tramp stay in my house and she fucked my man. I said 'help yourself' but I didn't mean my damn husband!"

"Un huh?" Megan asked, inviting her to get to the point. She let out a bored yawn at her mundane job.

"And I kilt both they asses!" she shot back and dug out the murder weapon from her purse. The precinct exploded in activity when the gun came out.

"Gun!" a cop shouted and out came twenty more guns. "Drop it! Put the gun down! Drop it!"

The scorned woman scrunched her face in confusion at all the activity. The confusion caused her to turn with the gun and get gunned down. Four of the twenty guns pointed at her discharged sending 12 rounds into her body. She did the Harlem shake as the rounds tore into her torso. The woman dropped dead right on the spot and stared up at her with dead eyes.

Megan sat there blinking rapidly trying to process seeing the woman killed right before her eyes. The rest of the day was a blur of statements and paperwork. Ultimately the recording would tell the story of the woman with the gun. She was still in shock when she was taken into an office to be questioned and coached on the right answers.

"So, she threatened you with the gun... " the investigator led hoping to lead Megan statement.

"No. She was showing me the gun she used to kill her husband and sister. She caught them fuc... " she said before getting cut off.

"No, she threatened you with the gun," he repeated and backed the video up to the part when she pulled the gun. "And your fellow officers saved your life by..."

A brief silence followed as the two stared at each other. The investigator saw a ray of hope shine through as she began to get it. He nodded his head as she came around.

"Engaging the suspect and neutralizing the threat," she said nodding along with him. A broad smile spread across the captain's face seeing that she understood.

"Good girl," he cheered stopping just short of patting her on her head. "Make sure you report to patrol briefing in the morning!"

• • • •

MEGAN DROVE HOME IN a fog of mixed emotions. She just saw a confused woman gunned down and then lied on her. The shock of seeing her baby sister riding her husband backwards was too much on her. She wasn't a killer but they pushed her. She went down to the cops for guidance and got turned into a corpse. All three lay side by side in the morgue like a macabre ménage a trio.

"Tuh," Megan huffed indignantly. Yeah she lied and helped cover up the wrongful death but it got her from behind the desk. One thing she learned from her mother is that you have to look out for your damn self. She lifted her head high and crossed over the bridge into the Bronx.

"Five-0! Oh wait, that's just Megan," a teen called out as Megan walked through the courtyard in her uniform. Technically she didn't have to come this way since she parked in front but then no one would get to see her in her uniform.

"See you graduated, huh?" she asked the newest dope boy. Someone went to jail so he made his way over from the monkey bars to the trap.

"I ain't doing shit," he said raising his hands in surrender. He gave himself away when he cut his eyes over to the bushes.

"So that's not your stash over there in the brown paper bag?" she asked cocking her head curiously. Megan had declared war on drugs but this was a green zone since she and her family had to live here. She didn't make any arrests but demanded to be respected just like Officer Johnson was when it was his beat.

"Huh?" he asked with his eyes wide. Megan shook her head and walked off as his friends laughed at him.

"Sup, Megan," Na-Na cheered when she made her way passed the thot section.

"Chilling," she replied outwardly while internally shaking her head. The girl was only a couple years older than her but had her third baby in her belly. Megan pressed on and went into the pissy stairwell for the sprint up to her apartment. She smiled when her grandmother's fried chicken won out all the other smells in the hallway. She could smell the jerk, curry and African spices but they weren't competing with Dianne's fried chicken.

"Sup, yo," little Jax greeted when his big sister walked in. He adored Megan even if she still wouldn't call him by his name.

"Sup, Roscoe. Homework?" she asked coming to look over his shoulder. He was a studious kid just like she was except he went out to play with the other project kids once his homework was done. This was all he knew so he couldn't turn his nose up.

"Yeah. Almost done, then me and Mike-mike gonna play ball," he replied as he wrapped up. She annoyed him by patting his head like a puppy and turned the corner into the kitchen.

"How was work?" Dianne asked sticking her cheek out for some sugar and getting some.

"Muah! It was great and guess what?" she asked but was too excited to share to wait on her guess. "I got transferred to patrol! Starting tomorrow, I'm on the streets."

"Oh, that's nice," her grandmother replied minus any trace of enthusiasm. Safe desk work suited her just fine over the danger of the streets.

"Don't worry, grandma. I'm trained and ready," she said trying to ease her fears. She stole the phrase from Officer Johnson and they both knew it. They both knew how that turned out as well. The mood slowed to crawl as the heavy words hung in the air.

"So when is that chocolate bar coming back over here?" Dianne asked to change the subject. He was going away to school soon so he was there almost every night and was closing in on getting some pussy.

"He's supposed to come over tonight, but I don't know? I'm going on patrol in the morning so I probably better get some sleep, huh?" she answered and asked. She twisted her lips thinking how good she slept and busting a strong nut from his strong hand.

"Well, maybe just for a little while."

"Yeah, a little while," Dianne laughed and fixed the plates for dinner. "Jax, come eat."

• • • •

"I'M CUMMING," GERALD warned in a whisper. His body told her before his mouth did so Megan had the rag ready. She covered the tip of his dick just before it began to spasm and spit.

"Dang," she marveled at the throbs and spasm as he came. She kept tugging and stroking as his legs kicked beneath them.

"Your turn," he said eager to play in her pussy. He had to go first because she would get sleepy after she got off.

"I'm good. I gotta get up early," she sighed. "Want me to drive you home?"

"And who's going to drive you home?" he shot back like always. "I got a test so..."

"Bye," she sang to his dick and waved as he put it away. They kissed some more at the door before she let him out. She hit the window to watch over him as he walked through the projects. The stickup kids gave a nod and let him keep his shit. Megan was sound asleep by the time he reached the subway.

Chapter 2

"**F**reeze! No, wait, OK. Show me your hands!" Megan practiced as she drove to work. Her keen eye spotted drug deals, prostitution and felons in possession of firearms everywhere she looked. She couldn't wait to hit the streets so she could make some arrest. "Do not move!"

Megan never attended the morning briefings since she was just a secretary up until now. She didn't know quite what to expect but didn't expect quite what she got. She walked into the briefing room early and took a seat right up front so she wouldn't miss anything. Soon other cops filed in by ones and twos. Most went to partake of the coffee and donuts provided by the city. Megan scanned the room wondering which on of the vets she would be paired with. It almost reminded her of high school with some kids talking amongst themselves while the teacher tried to teach.

She blushed and blinked when her eyes met the hazel eyes of the precinct's pretty boy, Floyd. His nickname of 'Pretty Boy Floyd' wasn't very creative but it fit. She avoided the high yellow cutie like the plague. It was wise because if he did have the plague half the women in the precinct would have it since he had sex with them. The other half was unfuckable due to weight or being just plain ugly. He gave a wink that made her vagina clench to hold on to her virginity.

"Good morning," the captain greeted as he entered the room. "You guys welcome Officer Robinson to patrol."

Megan cheesed widely as she accepted the greetings and murmurs of her coworkers. It was brief since she wasn't new to the precinct, but new to patrol. The captain went through his normal spiel and showed pictures of wanted criminals to be on the look out for. Megan noticed most cops weren't even paying attention to him as he spoke.

"Sorry I'm late," Officer Pascal said as he came in. The captain didn't even look his way but Megan did.

She vaguely remembered meeting the man when her dad brought her to work to show her off. She did know of him and his antics from around the precinct. The one time detective was so incompetent he was busted back down the ranks until he ended up back in a patrol car where he started twenty-five ago. His uniform looked like he slept in it but his eyes looked like he hadn't slept at all. Half of whatever he ate for breakfast adorned his shirt and some was stuck in his thick mustache. He, too, missed the briefing when he made a beeline to the coffee and donuts.

"OK, guys. Be safe out there!" the captain said in closing. He darted towards the door so he could look at some barely legal naked teens online.

"Uh, excuse me, captain. Who am I partnered with?" Megan asked catching him before he could get away. She pointed at herself and rocked on her heels in anticipation.

"Huh? Oh yeah, you're riding with Pascal. Be safe out there," he blurted and stormed off for a date with his palm.

"Pascal!" she shrieked in sheer horror. She'd seen the bumbling cop screw up a hundred things in a hundred ways in the year she'd been here.

"Huh?" Pascal asked hearing his name snapped him from his sleep. Being an overweight slob gave him symptoms of narcolepsy where he could fall asleep at the drop of a dime.

"Sheesh, let's ride," she sighed, eager to hit the streets and clean them up.

. . . .

"I'LL DRIVE," PASCAL offered when they reached the motor pool and found their car.

"You sure?" she insisted since he looked sleepy and smelled like alcohol. She wanted to take the keys from his hand and go around to the drivers side.

"Girl I was driving a squad car before your dad met your mom," he said truthfully. The truth didn't prevent him from backing into a pole as he pulled out. The minor accident didn't even register and he pulled out of the garage.

"You was partners with my dad?" she asked as the cruised the streets of Harlem.

"For about a year when we both started. Good guy that Rohan," he reminisced. As he spoke she scanned the block and saw a drug transaction taking place. She'd seen enough hand to hand sales from her projects window to spot one a mile away.

"Pull over. That guy just made a sale," she said looking back as they drove by.

"Who? Ole Jose? Yeah he peddles nickel bags of weed. Hardly worth chasing him down the block. The weed is not even that good," he said as he kept driving and talking.

"Now that's something that needs investigation!"

"Donuts?" she asked as he pulled to a stop in front of a donut shop. She shook her head and followed him inside.

"Not just donuts. Bear claws! And they comp us," he said in a whisper. Megan pursed her lips at him while noticing the perturbed look on the clerk's face.The woman turned and said something in Spanish to the cook that made them both giggle.

"They make mines special," he bragged. "Want one?"

"I know," she replied since she spoke Spanish fluently. She didn't like spit on her food so she declined. "No thanks."

"They love me around here. I got a few spots around the beat that feed me. You don't have to spend a dime when your with me. One of the perks of being a cop!" he said eating his spit-laced pastry.

Megan remembered Officer O'Neil's words that all cops get something free. She crossed her arms and balled up her face in defiance, determined to never be on the take. Her mind flashed to her dead mentor's memoirs. Then shook the thought to finally read them out of her head. She had the pretty diary since her death but still held a grudge and wouldn't open it.

"Speaking of dirty cops, did you know Officer Jackson? The one who killed my dad?" she asked. Pascal frowned wondering what he missed about dirty cops. He was pretty sure he hadn't fallen, but then he could have. It wouldn't be the first time.

"Yeah, good kid. Had potential," Pascal admitted honestly. "Jax made a big splash when he hit patrol. He made so many drug arrest he made detective quicker than anyone in his academy class..."

No cop comes in the door seeking to be a bad cop. Something happens somewhere, somehow and turns them over to the dark side. It could be drugs or pussy, which is a drug in its own but mostly its money. All cops take money in one way or the other. Even the fat man behind the wheel was on the take with all the free food he collected all day.

Megan took her own lessons from the story. One, that a ton of arrests was the key to getting promoted. Some cops spend decades spinning their wheels literally and figuratively in a patrol car. They made more money than arrest and never got promoted. She could have made three arrests by lunch but her partner wouldn't pull over. He drove around, talking and eating free food. The day ended without a single arrest but Officer Pascal gained three pounds from pasta, pizza, donuts and hotdogs but didn't pay a dime.

"So, how was your first day?" the captain inquired when they returned at the end of the shift.

"Ugh!" Megan replied and stormed off to the locker room. Most cops showered and changed before leaving but Megan preferred to wait until she got home. Just like her dad she loved her uniform and loved being seen in it.

"Piece of cake," Officer Pascal said with a conspiratorial wink. He was ordered to keep her safe and away from the action and did just that.

• • • •

"SO HOW WAS YOUR FIRST day?" Dianne tried to ask as Megan as barged in the apartment. She didn't even see or hear the woman as she came inside the apartment.

"Ugh!" she repeated and stormed down the hall. She ignored her brother when she went into the room they still shared. He saw her gathering items for her shower and took the hint. He paused his game and left to give her some privacy.

Megan would often relieve herself with a good nut in the shower but was too frustrated to enjoy herself by playing with herself. The hot water and aromatic body wash helped and she felt better when she got out. She felt even better when she smelled dinner when she returned from her room.

"I didn't know you were here, grandmother?" she sang and kissed her cheek.

"So how was your first day?" she asked again as Megan reached over her shoulder and grabbed a piece of chicken.

"Ugh!" she repeated then repeated the day's events. Dianne didn't share her frustration about her sorry partner since he would keep her out of trouble. Little did Dianne know, nothing could keep her out of trouble. She was her mother's daughter too and some of Michelle was in her, as well. The only difference was when and how it would surface. After dinner, Megan retired to the room to read her former friend's diary.

"All cops take money. Hmph!" she huffed at the memory and turned the page.

Dear diary, I don't know about undercover work. These guys got me shaking my ass like bait for the dope boys. Sure it's easy work because they tell you all their business but they all wanna fuck. I got a man and these niggas pulling their nasty ass dicks out on me.

Today this dude stuffed a wad of cash in my pockets to get in my panties. I tried to turn it in but Sarge said keep it! 'All cops take money', he said. I took it alright. Took it straight to the closest church and dropped it in the mail slot.

"Hmph, so how you got all that shit in your apartment?" Megan fussed at her dead friend's memory and tossed the diary aside. She blinked a few times before the sandman came and whisked her away.

Chapter 3

"Good morning," the captain greeted and started his morning briefing. As usual Megan was the only one paying attention.

As usual Pascal was late again and headed straight for the donuts and coffee. The stain spot in the same spot on his shirt said it was the same one from the previous day. She shook her head, which brought her eye to eye with Pretty Boy Floyd. He had been staring at her curly ponytail waiting for her to turn around. She was the only fuckable woman in the precinct he hadn't fucked yet. He shot a quick wink and flashed his smile. Megan snarled in return to his wink and turned back around.

"OK, we have a B.O.L.O for Raheem Jenkins. A regular Jessie James sticking up everything moving. He shot an old lady in her leg last night so it's time to relocate him upstate," Captain said in closing. The stickup kid was fine as long as he was robbing and shooting niggers but now that he attacked a white woman he had to go. No one paid him much attention until he said, "Be safe out there."

"Thanks, captain!" Megan cheered but she was the only one. The cops filed out and got in their squad cars. She let out a sigh as Pascal squeezed behind the wheel. As usual they were the last ones to their car and last out of the garage.

"You sure you don't need me to drive? You look sleepy," she offered. It was a true lie because he did look sleepy but that's not why she wanted to drive.

"Nah, I got it. I can catch some z's at the red lights," he chuckled as if it was a joke. It wasn't because she had to wake him up for green lights several times the day before. Pascal would just pick up right where he left off with whatever story he was telling.

"Yeah," she said and got back into the diary. She was amazed at what undercover work actually entailed. Pascal rambled on in between stops to eat but she missed most of what he was saying as she read. Her eyes went wide as she read about Officer O'Neil's undercover adventures. They were on their third lunch of the day when she looked up from the diary and locked eyes with Raheem Jenkins.

"Ooh, ooh! Look! That's the guy?"

"Yup," he replied after a glance but kept driving by. "There's a pizza joint up here that's got some killer calzones!"

11

"But..." she complained.

Raheem locked in on the cop car and watched them until they were gone, then turned back to his crap game. Megan knew the only way she was going to make detective was by making arrests. She glanced over at Pascal and saw her future. Stuck in a patrol car twenty-five years eating calzones and canolis fat as fuck and decided, "Fuck that!"

"Hey! Where you going?" Pascal pleaded when the door flew open and his partner took off. He slammed his fat foot down on the brake to stop the car.

"Seven, ugh!" Raheem said as he shook the dice and tossed them on the sidewalk. They came up sevens but he didn't get to collect his prize.

"Oh shit!" one of the dice shooters exclaimed as Megan came flying through the air.

"What?" Raheem asked and turned to see what his friend saw just as Megan landed on him. She was only a fine, firm 140 but her momentum was strong enough to take the larger man down. They both crashed on the concrete, dice and money.

"You, are, under...arrest!" she said as she struggled to put the cuffs on him. It was easier said than done because Raheem didn't want to go to jail.

"Yo, get off me!" he demanded and wriggled out of her grip. He got free and they both scrambled to their feet. His eyes went wide when they both stood and he saw it was a lady cop. Not just a lady cop, but a gorgeous lady cop with plump breast and a fat ass.

"Sup, ma? Be easy."

"Get your hands up!" she demanded from behind her gun. She took a shooter's stance ready to shoot. Raheem was a shooter himself and recognized that glint in her eye and knew she would gun him down. He was armed but she had the drop on him and he knew it.

"Be easy, ma. We good." he said raising his hands and lowering himself to his knees. He decided to try his luck with a judge instead of the 40 caliber aimed at his face.

"I got him!" Pascal shouted when he finally arrived on the scene. He threw his weight on his back and cuffed him up. "What the heck did you do that for?"

"Because I'm a cop. That's what cops do!" she shouted back. It dawned on her that she just made her first arrest and a smile spread on her face.

"At least I got bagged by a pretty bitch!" Raheem bragged as he was stuffed in the back seat. He flirted the whole ride down to get booked in at the precinct. "Yo, you gonna hold a nigga down? Write, and come visit?"

Megan's mind drifted away to her mother doing time upstate. Not only did she not write or visit her, she wouldn't even open any of the letters she received once a week. She didn't look at it as if she was holding a grudge. She just didn't fuck with her.

"Good job!" the captain nodded when the wanted fugitive was brought in. Megan cheesed as she got a round of applause for her first arrest.

"Thank you, captain. Can I have a word with you, captain?" she asked.

"Ummm..." he said instead of the 'no' he wanted to say. He was in the middle of his afternoon porn and she wanted to talk. "Sure?"

"I want another partner! I know you stuck me with Pascal to keep me away from the action but I'm a cop! I want to be in the action!" she insisted.

"OK, OK," the captain gave in and gave up. He saw then this would be a long conversation so he let her have it. "You'll have a new partner in the morning!"

"Than..." she began to say but he was already gone. She clapped, bounced and twirled until she saw Raheem staring at her from the holding cell. He winked and blew her a kiss. Megan scrunched her face up like a girl and left.

Megan made two more arrests by the end of the day despite Pascal's best efforts not to do any work. She didn't mind and did most of the work. She ran one drug dealer down and tackled him. Then spotted a pickpocket in progress and put the cuffs on him. She did all the paperwork without complaints, just like her father would. Everyone was saying how she was just like her father. No one paused to think that her father was dead.

· · · ·

"SO, HOW WAS WORK?" Gerald asked once Megan returned from checking on her family. She made sure her brother and grandmother were sleeping soundly so they could make out. This would be their last time together for six months until he returned.

"Great! I made three arrests today!" she replied while pulling her panties off so he could play in her box. He looked around cautiously and whipped out the wood. He was already rock hard in anticipation. They usually took turns pleasing each other but tonight they engaged in a 29. The PG version of a 69, using hands instead of mouths.

They leaned in and began to kiss while fondling each other. She yanked his erection up and down while he rubbed her vagina. He grew harder and thicker while she produced a puddle from her pussy.

"Put your finger in it," she decided when he took her nipple in his mouth. He eagerly complied and slid his middle finger inside of her. "Sss."

"Dang!" he said feeling how tight she was around his finger. "I'm ready."

"To?" she asked even though she knew. She was ready too but wanted to hear him say it.

"To make love to you," he announced confidently. They locked eyes and agreed with a nod. He stood so she could lay on the sofa. She thought about throwing one leg on the back of the sofa like she'd seen her grandmother do with Officer Johnson but shook the thought away. Luckily for her because she wasn't ready for all that yet.

She realized that when Gerald dropped his pants and she saw his dick sticking straight out in the air. He laid between her legs and kissed her again. He reached down and rubbed the head of his dick between her slippery lips.

"Mmm," she moaned and braced herself to lose her virginity. Would have too if not for the giggle from the hallway. "Brad!"

"Y'all nasty! I'm telling!" Jax snickered. Gerald popped up and scrambled to pull his pants up. In his haste, he zipped some dick skin up in his zipper.

"Yeoow!" he screamed and went down to his knees, making little Jax laugh even louder.

"What the hell is going on out here?" Dianne demanded as she came out in her nightgown with old titties swinging, giving Jax something else to laugh about. She hit the light and blinked them into view.

"Nothing. Why you ask?" Megan asked calmly despite Gerald doubled over trying to free his dick skin and her panties laying on the floor. She tried to pose naturally as if nothing were wrong while tears streamed down his face.

"Boy, did you catch the bark from your wood? Come on, let me see," the lady laughed. Dianne knew how to get a dick out a zipper in more ways than one. The request was purely clinical but she still wanted to see what he was working with. "Let's see what you working with. Mmhm, yes lawd."

"Grandma!" Megan reeled when her grandmother leaned in to inspect the damage.

"Damn!" Dianne pronounced with a grimace when she saw just how much skin he caught in the teeth of the zipper. "How in the hell did you do all that? You might need some stitches. Jax, go get some bandaids and rubbing alcohol."

"Stitches? Alcohol!" Gerald pleaded and winced. Jax was black in a flash handing over the medical supplies

"So it won't get infected. Now hold still, take a deep breath. On the count of three. One, two..." she advised then surprised him on the two count.

"Yeoow!" Gerald screamed when she snatched the zipper down. That screech was nothing compared to the one that followed when she hit him with the alcohol.

"Yeeeooow!"

Jax snickered at him until his grandmother chased him off. She put two bandaids on the teeth marks the zipper left behind. Gerald bounced from foot to foot as she attended to his mauled man meat. Megan held her hands to her mouth in shock.

"You fine. Now go home," Dianne announced once she finished first aid to his penis. Gerald looked at Megan like he wanted to say something but grandma wasn't hearing it. "Home!"

"Call me," she pleaded as he departed. She attempted to leave too once the door closed. "Welp, work in the morning. Good night."

"Girl, sit yo' ass down," Dianne said pointing at the same sofa she almost lost her virginity on.

"Huh?" she asked looking up after sitting down. She tried to discreetly kick her panties under the sofa but Dianne saw her and shook her head.

"OK, first. How you having sex in the living room with every one in the house? Anyone could have come out. This how you want your little brother to see you?"

"Um?" Megan said thinking about how many times she'd seen or heard her and Officer Johnson having sex on this same sofa. It sure beat the rooftop or staircase the other girls were fucking in. "But we didn't do it. I'm still a virgin."

"I'm still a virgin," Dianne mocked, "Girl, your panties on the floor. He had his dick out. You wasn't about to be a virgin much longer. And, I don't see know condom!"

"I..." Megan said and stopped. She was so caught up in the moment she forgot all about protection. She realized how close she came to potential disaster and accepted her scolding. "Yes, ma'am."

"Yeah well, I hope you both learned a lesson," she concluded and lifted herself off the sofa. She mumbled her way down the hall and into bed.

Meanwhile Megan was too hot and bothered to sleep so she got into the shower. She masturbated under the hot water to relieve herself. Now that her cat was out the bag it would be hard to put back in. It was going to be a long six months.

Chapter 4

I'll never forget that feeling when my mouth filled with salty semen from some drug dealer's dick. I honestly thought about my man as this man ejaculated in my mouth. Raul would never understand I did what I had to do to make my case. Once we flip this clown he'll rat out his connect. I'll fuck him too if necessary to build a case. When I finally reach my target, the infamous Junior Ruiz, I'll be able to write my own ticket. That's Captain O'Neil, thank you very much...

"Eww!" Megan grimaced and covered her mouth so no imaginary cum could enter it. She thought about the thick globs of baby batter Gerald skeeted when she jacked him off and grimaced again. "Not in the mouth though!"

"Huh?" Jax asked from across the room making her realize she was thinking aloud. He popped up and looked over to his sister.

"Ain't nobody talking to you! Go back to sleep." she fussed back at him.

"I was sleep until you started talking!" he shot back and shut her up.

"Ugh! Whatever! I'm going to take a shower," she said and rolled out of her twin bed. She made a decent salary and had plenty saved plenty but the thought of moving into her own apartment never dawned on her. She would say she had to take care of her grandmother and little brother but they took care of her too.

"Again?" he asked since he had to give up the room earlier for her to shower. She always commandeered the room for an hour after a shower to dress and primp.

"Yes, again!" she shot back slightly embarrassed at what she had in mind. The diary had her hot and horny and she needed to relieve herself a second time. "Wish Gerald was here."

A few hours later, alarms began to ring around the apartment to start the day. The night shift of addicts and dealers all went home as the law-abiding citizens began to move about. Dianne's internal clock woke her an hour earlier so she could cook breakfast for her family.

"Come on, guys. Let's move it!" she called out once her job was done. Breakfast was cooked and lunches were packed.

Jax knew to get in the one bathroom and get out before his sister did. He was still too young to care about his appearance so it didn't take long. Megan on the other hand spent an hour just to look plain. She was all girl and loved to be cute but wanted to be taken serious as a police officer. Her ass was just as fat as her female counterparts but she subdued hers with loose uniform pants and bulletproof vest.

"Thanks, grandmother," Megan said accepting her breakfast smoothie and peanut butter and jelly lunch.

"What she said," Jax said for his sweet cereal and same lunch as his big sister. The family said their goodbyes and went their separate ways.

• • • •

"NOT IN THE MOUTH THOUGH. Eww," Megan repeated as Officer O'Neil's diary played in her mind. As interesting as it was, she was ready to get to the part where she went wrong. The part when she went from good cop to bad cop. The woman had an abundance of cash and a new car before she died. Cops got a decent wage but not enough for all that.

She found a spot near the precinct, parked and walked over. Early as usual the briefing room was empty when she arrived. She took her regular seat up front and waited.

Pretty Boy Floyd winked as he sauntered in and took a seat. Once the room filled, the captain entered and got started. He recognized Megan once more for apprehending the wanted man. No one paid attention to most of what he had to say until he dropped a bomb on them.

"We are reassigning everyone today. Listen up for your new partners," he said then paused for the moans and groans. Some teams had been partners for years and had bonded. Others had their money making rackets going strong and didn't want to break them up. In the end it was all for nothing since Megan and a Chinese cop were the only changes. Ming Chang just got saddled with 300 pounds of dead weight named Pascal while she got his partner.

"Robinson and Floyd. Be safe out there," he concluded and rushed off to his porn.

Megan frowned and looked around the room for another Floyd. She just knew there had to be another besides the pretty boy. She shook her head when the room emptied except for the two of them.

"So, I finally got you to myself," he said flashing that pussy getting smile of his. He'd been openly flirting with her since the day she arrived but literally couldn't get the time of day. He tried that too, asking what time it was just to get her to speak to him. She would simply point at the clock and keep it moving.

"I'm here to work. That's it. Now, can we go lock up some bad guys?" she shot back all business like. She made sure to avoid eye contact when she spoke to him. Afraid the hazel gems would see right through her.

Floyd nodded and raised his hands in surrender. There was no need to push the issue since he did indeed have her all to himself. He led the way out to the motor pool to claim their vehicle. There was no discussion about who would drive since he got in and slid behind the wheel. Megan twisted her lips but kept quiet. Pretty boy or not, Floyd made a ton of arrests and would certainly move up the ranks.

"So, how you like being a cop?" Floyd asked as they began their patrol. They would cruise the same Harlem streets as she and Pascal but now she could actually work.

"I don't like it. I love it. It's all I ever wanted to be. My dad was a cop. Worked this same precinct. Patrolled these same streets," she said fondly. She knew most partners bonded due to the life and death missions and hoped they would too.

"What's your favorite position?" he tossed out casually. It was so random she wasn't sure if she actually heard him correctly.

"Huh?" she asked with a curious smile stuck on her face. She was pretty sure she heard him but the words didn't make much sense.

"From the back, face to face? You look like the cowgirl type," he decided with a head nod. "You like to ride it? Turn around and ride backwards?"

"Bruh, what the fuck is wrong with you? I'm a cop! Not a thot!" she fumed. Would have read him the riot act if a young man hadn't caught her eye. He had the usual duck waddle of dudes with baggy jeans but he favored one leg with a slight limp. To the untrained eye he looked like he sprained an ankle perhaps, but Megan's eyes were trained.

"Gun."

"Where? Who?" Floyd asked darting his eyes in his turning head. He scanned all hands for a handgun but didn't see any. "I don't see a gun?"

"Red shirt, blue jeans. He's strapped," she assured him as they rode by. The guy cut his eyes and the squad car and turned up a side block.

"I don't see no gun?" Floyd frowned, still checking his hands. They were both empty save the menthol he took tokes on.

"In his waistband. Trust me, he's carrying," she pleaded. She got scolded real good yesterday after the pats on the back for jumping out of a moving car so she stayed put.

"If you say so," he sighed and pulled off. He circled around the block and whipped up on the subject. The man didn't see the cops until they jumped out on him. He turned to run but they were on his ass.

Megan was slightly impressed by her partner's speed and strength. He exploded out of the car and closed the distance between him and the perp in a few long strides.

"What's up? What I do?" the man screamed as he was quickly subdued and cuffed.

"How's about carrying a concealed weapon?" she asked as she removed a large semiautomatic pistol from his pants.

"You planted that!" he shouted. It was a nice try but the dash cam would say otherwise. The partners gave a high five to celebrate their first arrest.

"What'll you got? X-ray vision or something? How'd you see that gun?" Floyd asked once they were back in the car. Megan paused and thought about how many times she'd seen how many dudes put guns in their pants from her project's window. She observed the difference of how they walked before and after. Armed and unarmed, pockets, waist or small of their back, each had a different swag.

"Um, yeah I do. Except lead. I can't see through lead or if some kryptonite is around. It zaps my powers," she said with a completely straight face. So seriously the dumb ass in their back seat believed it.

"Yo! You super girl, ma?" he asked wide eye with delight. Now he had a doozy of a story to tell when he got to Rikers Island. Megan just shook her head and ignored him.

"Can you see through pants, too?" Floyd asked seductively. She ignored that too and looked out the window.

• • • •

"WANNA GET SOME LUNCH?" Floyd asked after they booked in their third suspect before noon. Megan saw him make a drug deal and they swooped in and scooped him up like a eagle does its dinner.

"I brought a Caesar salad," she replied and reached into the back seat to retrieve her lunch bag. Floyd turned and tried to look at her ass in the baggy uniform pants. She came up and saw him looking at her and shook her head once more.

"You need to eat a real meal so you can fill them pants up," he suggested. She dug into her salad as if he hadn't even spoken. "I like my salad tossed personally. You ever have your salad tossed?"

Megan lifted a finger indicating him to wait as she chewed the mouth full of lettuce and etceteras. She swallowed and washed it down with a swig of water so she could reply.

"One, I'm a cop. Two, no I have never had my butt licked and doubt I would want to. Third, I have a boyfriend. Fourth, are you going to make sexual references all day every day?" she rattled off. There was a brief silence while he processed the question and gave his answer.

"Yes. It's what I do. Make a lot of arrests too but the banter fills the time," he replied. It wasn't his fault they stuck a chick in the car with him and saw no reason to change up.

"Well..." Megan paused. She didn't quite expect his candor and a really couldn't argue with his reasoning. She'd been a cop long enough to be immune to the crass, locker room banter. "I still have a boyfriend."

"If he ain't tossing your salad, he don't really love you," he lied. Licking assholes has no bearing on love. Dogs lick each others ass all the time and it doesn't mean they love each other. Megan just shook her head and sighed.

He was right about one thing. They made a shit load of arrests. By the end of their first day, they apprehended five suspects and she changed her mind about planning to change partners.

Chapter 5

ear diary, so I'm on to a mid level dealer named Cortez. It's funny how I used to look down on female cops who fuck their way to the top. I said I would never do that. Hard work would pay off and I would get there off my merits. Now I'm fucking dope boys for info and locking them up.

I could like Cortez in another life. He's handsome, funny and ate my pussy so well my legs shook for two days. They were shaking the next day in briefing under the table. LOL. Fucked up part is that its just a matter of time until he stops taking no for an answer and wants me to return the favor. I'll fuck him if I have to but I hate doing this to Raul. He deserves better but I'm too selfish to let him go. An undercover lady cop really doesn't need a man.

Cortez gave me a pocketbook full of cash. Dirty, nasty, filthy, bloody, drug money. I gave it to a bag lady that same day. You should have seen her face. My little sister, Megan, swears she wants this. I swear she couldn't handle it. She too nice, too sweet, too....

"Can too!" Megan fussed at her friend's memory. She was moved to be called her little sister but took the rest as a challenge. Anytime anyone told her she couldn't do anything she set out to prove them wrong. "And you still ain't said how you got that car and that furniture and all the money!"

"Good morning!" Captain greeted as he entered to start the briefing. Megan snapped the diary closed and paid close attention. Floyd paid attention to her neck, hair and lips. She could play hard to get all she wanted but he was determined to tap that. He had six months and time was ticking. As a result, he missed most of the briefing as he pictured different positions to fuck her in. "Be safe out there!"

"You ready to lock up some bad guys?" Megan asked eagerly as they walked to the squad car. Floyd fell back so he could watch her ass as they walked. Baggy pants couldn't quite hide all that ass like she intended. He didn't hear a word she said trying to trace her panty lines. Megan felt his eyes on her ass and turned. "Bruh?"

"My bad, Robinson. You ever been ate out from the back?" he apologized then immediately contradicted it.

"No!" Megan shot back. She felt her face flush as she blushed at the very thought of it. She heard enough about getting ate out to know it was a wonderful thing. Once again her panties got moist. She had began wearing panty liners to sop up all the juice he produced everyday. "Can we just go arrest some bad people without all the sex talk?"

"Absolutely not!" he laughed making her vagina quiver with his baritone laughter. "I mean sure, we're gonna lock people up, but I'm gonna talk about sex! It's what I do!"

Floyd kept his words about both. They led the precinct in arrests for four months straight but he never let up on the sexual innuendos. He was the king of the double entendres. They bantered and bickered between slapping the cuffs on perps. If Megan had a dollar for every time he soaked her panties she would have quite a few dollars. It took five months before she decided to give him a taste of his own medicine. He could dish it out so she wanted to see if he could take it. Gerald was almost home and she was home free. She planned to throw her virginity into his face as soon as he stepped off his plane.

"How'd you sleep last night?" Floyd asked as he pulled from the garage for a day of patrol. It seemed innocuous but he had a sexual comeback for whatever she replied. Good sleep or bad sleep was somehow related to his dick. He was as witty as he was handsome and she couldn't and wouldn't deny that. She would, however, deny the fact that his face replaced Gerald's a couple of times when she played with herself.

"Not good. I was restless so I had to masturbate a few times to calm down," she whined. She struggled not to laugh when the car swerved in response.

"Huh? Why, why, you pl, played in yo, yo, yo, your p, pussy?" he stuttered, trying to drive and look over at her. He ran a red light, narrowly avoiding a nasty accident.

"Yeah, I do almost everyday. I have to do it in the shower because it gets so wet. So, so wet." she purred and felt herself actually get wet. It was nothing compared to what Floyd was going through. His dick was so hard it hurt being confined in his pants. She peeped down in his lap and saw the bulge in his pants. "I'll mess up my sheets if I do it in my bed. It be juice everywhere!"

"Shit!" he exclaimed. He gripped the wheel tightly and shifted in his seat. He wracked his brain in search of some words that could get himself inside of her. He was ready to offer cold, hard cash to get inside that hot box. "Let me see it! Come on, I know you got a picture of it?"

"Yo, look at it." she said pointing at an obvious prostitute as she sauntered up the sidewalk. Megan squinted at the woman's face and saw she was no woman. She was no he either but she needed to know. "How old is she?"

"I don't know," Floyd said. It was hard for him to tell since he was looking at the fat ass cheeks bouncing beneath the purple boy shorts. They both watched as she switched over to a Lexus and paid her pimp the price for her pussy.

"That must be her bitch ass pimp," Megan practically growled of the flashy young man in the flashy car. Back in the days pimps looked like pimps. Now they looked like rappers. He broke another law when he lifted a smoldering blunt to his mouth and took a pull. It was probable cause to lock his ass up.

"You get him and I'll get the girl," Floyd suggested as the girl dipped into a tenement building to turn another trick. The teen was damn near a magician the way she could make erections disappear down her throat.

"Bet!" she said as he pulled around the block. He pulled to a stop behind the Lexus and they both set off after their prey. Floyd walked briskly but with a slight limp from a hard dick in his pants. He entered the building a moment after the girl.

"Excuse me?" Megan sang politely as she stuck her head into the car's open window. He flashed his gold and diamond smile as he turned and choked on his weed smoke. She grimaced and pulled her face from the car when she smelled the cocaine burning inside the cigar along with the weed. She lived in the projects long enough to know the difference between good green and ugly brown weed by smell. She could also identify weed laced with coke and crack.

"Sup, officer?" he asked as he flipped the blunt out the other window. He flashed his expensive smile once more hoping it helped. It got him a stable of young girls to rent their vaginas and mouths to contribute to his campaign so it might get him out of a ticket for smoking weed.

"What's up is you have the right to remain silent. Anything you...shit!" she fussed when he bailed out the car and took off. Tried to that is because his baggy jeans and untied sneakers prevented him from getting too far. Megan came around and quickly ran him down. She tackled him to the street and wrestled to put the cuffs on him. He resisted but was weak from sitting around smoking weed and coke too much to put up too much of a fight.

Meanwhile Floyd eased into the building he saw the young prostitute enter. He scanned the empty lobby and withdrew his pistol. Gagging noises from the stairs sent him in that direction. He reached the first landing and saw the girl squatted in front of a man with his whole dick in his mouth.

"Shit!" the 'John' fussed when he saw the cop. The last thing he needed was to get arrested for solicitation. His wife would certainly divorce him plus he would probably go to jail since she was underaged.

"Shit is right! Now put your dick away and get out of here! You, don't move," he ordered him and then her. The young prostitute twisted her lips knowing what was coming next.

The 'John' compiled and rushed off down the stairs. Floyd looked down at the girl still squatted and the fat mound of pussy protruding in her short shorts. He looked left, right and left again as if crossing the street. Instead he crossed the line and pulled his penis. This wasn't the first cop cock she sucked so she got straight to work. Luckily for both he was so worked up from the sexual banter with his partner that it wouldn't take long.

"Get it," he grunted and exploded in her mouth a few minutes later. His knees buckled as she gulped down any evidence of this crime. "Now get out of here."

"Where's the girl?" Megan frowned when her partner came back empty handed. His eyes fluttered and he yawned from the relaxing blow job.

"Little girl was quick! She needs to go back to school and run track. Sup with this clown?" he asked trying to divert the attention from himself.

"Possession of marijuana, cocaine and some kind of pills," she replied feeling disappointed they weren't adding pimping and pandering to the list of charges. "Oh and a gun from under his seat."

"Good collar," he congratulated and raised his hand for a high five. She scrunched her face and slapped his hand before taking their latest capture to jail.

• • • •

"FLOYD, ROBINSON. IN my office!" the captain barked at the end of the morning briefing. Both looked at the other wondering what they did that got them both in trouble. They had made a ton of arrests in the nearly six months they'd been partners. Neither crossed the line by taking money or abusing suspects.

"What did you do?" Megan demanded squinting at him as the briefing room emptied leaving just the two of them alone.

"Me! What did you do?" he shot back. He thought about getting a few stray blow jobs on duty when he could get away with it. If his partner didn't know, no way the captain did. "Well, let's go see."

"My boyfriend comes home tomorrow and you get me fired!" she grumbled as she led the way to the captain's office. He fell back and let her go up the stairs before her so he could look up her ass. She knew it too and tossed it from side to side since it would be as close as he would ever get to it.

"Come in!" the captain barked in response to the knock on his door. He clicked off the porn site but left his penis out since it was beneath the desk. He saw no reason to put it up when he was just going to pull it right back out again as soon as they left.

"Yes sir!" Floyd barked and snapped to attention. Megan looked at him for a split second before copying his stance. He was crude but a good cop who loved being a cop.

"You two are off patrol after this shift," he barked as he ran his gaze back and forth between them. He snarled as if they disgusted him. If the kiddie porn on his computer didn't disgust him, nothing could.

"Yes sir!" Floyd barked obediently. His police pops taught him to obey orders no matter if you liked them or not. He didn't raise Megan though so she spoke up.

"But why? Why can't we patrol anymore? What did we do?" she asked with her voice cracking from disappointment.

"You made special duty is what you did. You both are being promoted to detective. Report to vice in the morning." he said smiling. Floyd smiled too but Megan frowned.

"I wanted to work narcotics like my dad!" she pouted. Floyd's head snapped down at her. He wanted to snatch her and drag her away before she made him change his mind.

"Like your dad, huh?" captain laughed. "Your dad worked vice for five years before making the narc squad."

"Oh! OK, then. Thank you," she smiled. They snapped back to attention and saluted. He waved them off and off they went.

"Yes!" Floyd cheered and wrapped Megan in his arms and off her feet. This time it was purely platonic joy but Megan melted at his touch. She was drunk from his smell and feel when he set her back down. "My bad, I..."

"No, its OK. We did it! We made detective!" she said, amazed at how it sounded. She wanted this for as long as she could remember and she made it.

"And we're going out to celebrate tonight. I'm not taking no for an answer!" he demanded. He'd been inviting her out on dates from day one but this was no date. This was a celebration.

"OK," she nodded in agreement. This was certainly an occasion to celebrate and her man would be home tomorrow.

Chapter 6

M egan smiled so hard on the drive home her cheeks began to hurt. She still had her uniform on because it would be her last time wearing it for a while. She wouldn't have to wear it again until the next cop funeral. She wouldn't put it up too far because there will always be more cop funerals.

"Sup y'all!" she greeted to the thots and toddlers on the bench as she breezed through the courtyard.

"Sup, Megan!" they sang back as she high fived them all in passing. She waved and greeted the dope boys next on her way to the building. Little did they know she was one step closer to locking them all up. Once she made it to narcotics she wouldn't spare anyone. It was her mission to remove drugs from society. She was still naive enough to believe it could be done.

"Hey, Leonard," Megan sang to her little brother as she came into the apartment. She playfully rubbed his head as he played him game with his friend.

"Stop! You messing up my waves!" he complained and ducked away.

"You ain't got no waves, boy!" she laughed and raked her fingers against the grain. He paused the game to run and brush them back in place.

"Them little girls sniffing around after him already!" Dianne explained his sudden attention to detail.

"Uh oh. You gonna be a great grandma soon!" she teased and kissed her cheek. "Ooh, guess what! I made detective is what! Starting Monday, I'm a detective!"

"Congratulations, baby!" she cheered and wrapped her granddaughter in her arms. She was doubly pleased at the good news. First because she knew she achieved a dream. Not many people from these projects got to achieve their dreams. Some did but most were stuck in the living nightmare of life in the projects. Second because she was naive enough to think detective work was somehow safer than patrol.

"Thank you, thank you," she said in mock arrogance and knocked imaginary dust from her shoulders.

"That's wonderful news! Now you won't be riding around looking for people to tackle anymore," she sighed in relief. The girl came home scuffed up with holes in her clothes at least once a week. Her deceased beau, Officer Johnson, used to often lament how the detectives didn't do shit but sit on their ass behind a desk. Patrol did all the work while the detectives got all the glory. That was just fine by Dianne.

"Thank you! Me and Floyd both made it. We're going out to celebrate!" she cheered on her way down the hall to shower and change.

"Pretty Boy Floyd?" grandma asked with concern in her voice. She could hear the attraction in Megan's voice when she complained about his constant come-ons. She may have turned him down but it was clear that she enjoyed the attention.

"Girl, stop!" Megan said twisting her lips at the look on the woman's face. "Ain't nothing about to happen. Besides, you know who comes home tomorrow!"

"OK... have fun," she said and left it alone.

Megan was a good girl and a grown woman who made good choices so she chose to bust a good nut in the shower to take the edge off before hanging out with her sexy partner. Both Gerald's and Floyd's handsome faces ran through her mind as she ran her fingers on her vagina. Gerald was in view when her knees buckled from the orgasm. She finished up and climbed out to dry off and get dressed.

"You OK?" Dianne asked from the living room when she heard the bathroom door open.

"Yeah, why?" Megan leaned around the corner and asked.

"You screamed in the shower. What you slipped or something?" she asked cracking little Jax completely up.

It wouldn't have been the first time she fell in the shower. Megan was completely embarrassed and slinked down the hall to her room.

She had nothing but large, comfortable cotton panties so she selected a pair. She matched a bra as closely as one who didn't buy matching sets could. She did select one of her two dresses that stopped just above her knees. They were as mini as her skirts got but she didn't want to wear one of her church dresses either. A pair of flats and purse completed the outfit and she was ready to go.

There were a few hours to kill so she filled them with her family. She played video games with her brother while chatting with her grandmother on the sofa behind them. Nine o'clock approached so she set out to the cop bar where all the cops from her precinct hung out. She parked down the block behind Floyd's late model BMW. He kept the older car cleaned and shiny making it look ten years newer.

"Hey!" Floyd yelled and waved to be seen and heard over the music and banter of the bar. She smiled and made her way over.

Oh my Megan thought to herself seeing him out of uniform. He was dangerously dapper in uniform but she had a thing for cops in uniform anyway. Most cops dressed like dorks in civilian clothes but not Pretty Boy Floyd. He looked even better in casual slacks and polo shirt. Her vagina contracted and throbbed when they embraced.

"Hey, Detective Floyd," she greeted when she pulled away from the friendly hug. Friendly or not she didn't put on a panty liner and didn't want to have a sponge between her legs all night.

"Detective Robinson," he returned and checked her out. Some female cops dressed like sluts to compensate wearing the manly uniform all day. Not Megan though. She dressed like a dork. A cute dork, but a dork nonetheless. "Drinks on me!"

"Um... OK," she replied since she never had a drink in her twenty-one years on the planet. She smoked weed once when her friend Officer O'Neil died. It made her giggle a little but other than that, she didn't get what all the hype was about. She shrugged and figured she could handle a drink or two.

"Two Long Island Iced Teas," Floyd ordered, holding two fingers up in case the bartender couldn't count.

"I grew up on Long Island!" Megan cheered. It was half true since she spent the first half of her life there. She watched as the man poured several different liquors and mixed them. The result looked just like iced tea and she knew she had this.

"To vice squad!" he cheered and raised his glass. Megan followed suite and raised hers too. They clinked glasses and put them to their mouth. Floyd locked eyes and chugged, encouraging her to do the same. She did and they both drained half the glass.

"Whew!" she grimaced when she realized it only looked like ice tea. The strong drink sent shivers through her soul. She was her mother's daughter and her mother was an addict. In fact Michelle was drinking homemade hooch and eating coochie in an upstate prison at that very moment.

"To getting out of patrol!" Floyd cheered and set off another toast. Two more toasts and the glasses were empty. He got the bartender's attention and held up those same two fingers. "Two more!"

Two more rounds and Megan was pissy drunk. When she began dancing in her chair that was Floyd's cue to take her home. He paid the tab and escorted the dancing machine towards the door.

"Let's hit the club! Turn up! Turn... oh shit!" she said and emptied the content of her stomach onto the sidewalk. Floyd held her hair so she wouldn't get vomit in it.

"Come on. Let's get you home," he comforted and escorted her up the street. She lifted her heavy head when she saw her car but he continued on to his. He got an eye full of fat crotch when he dumped her into his passenger seat.

Megan rocked and fell from side to side as he navigated the bumpy Manhattan streets. One of the most expensive places to live on the planet but the streets were like dirt roads. It proved to be too much for the remaining alcohol in Megan's belly.

"Arghh!" she groaned and spit up all over herself. Floyd shook his head at his freshly detailed interior. It still made out a lot better than her dress.

"Shit!" he fussed when they reached his apartment building. He was lucky enough to get a spot close to the door but unlucky to have to practically carry the inebriated woman up to his apartment. This was New York and no one batted an eye at the spectacle.

He put her over his shoulder and carried up the stairs. Using his free hand, he unlocked the door and went inside. He sat Megan against the bathroom door and turned the water on.

"Damn waste," he fussed as he pulled her soiled clothes off. Her frumpy underclothes gave him paused but, "Damn your ass is fine!"

As bad as he had been trying to get in her panties, he left them and the bra on and hoisted her into the bathtub. He did cop a feel here and there as he washed the alcohol smelling vomit from her face and body. He didn't bother drying her off and carried her into his room. He tossed her on the bed and stared down at her. His rock hard dick throbbed below as he ran his eyes over her curvy frame. He let out a heavy sigh at what would not be and climbed next to her on the bed. They were both sleep minutes later.

"Mmm," Megan moaned when she felt the hard body next to her when she stirred awake a couple hours later. She leaned into the hard dick and grinded her fat ass against it. She had this dream many a times. Only in the dream, an arm didn't wrap around her. A hand began to fondle her breast as she grinded against the rock hard dick. She spun over to look Gerald in his eyes and got the shock of her young life.

"Floyd! What the hell are you doing here?" she demanded. The 'here' she meant was her dream until she glanced around and saw where she was.

"I'm sorry! I didn't touch you!" Floyd vowed raising his hands as proof. There was an awkward silence as Megan tried to figure out what happened and what was happening. She was still tipsy so she leaned in and kissed him.

Floyd kissed her back then pulled away. He offered her a way out if she wanted. She didn't and kissed him again. He rolled her over and settled between her legs. Megan moaned and writhed beneath him as he grinded his dick on her soaked panties.

"Let me see this," he announced and dipped his face between her legs. It was better than Christmas when he pulled her panties off, unwrapping the brand new pussy. It would have been a crime not to eat that pussy and he was a cop after all.

"Ssss!" Megan hissed and arched her back all the way off the bed. Floyd put his hand on her stomach to hold her in place as he devoured her. She came so hard she shook the bed. That one was for her but he kept on eating her for himself. She came again and it was his turn.

Megan closed her eyes when he rose up and pulled out his dick. She popped one open to peep the penis then snapped it shut again. Floyd twisted his lips at the weird move. She didn't protest so he rubbed the head of his dick in the froth he left behind. She squeezed her eyes even tighter as he began to ease inside of her. She knew this was fucked up but wouldn't stop herself. Floyd stopped and frowned when he couldn't get inside of her. He actually looked down at it to make sure she didn't have panties on. He tried again and finally worked his way inside.

"Shit!!" Floyd fussed as the super tight, super wet vagina gripped his dick. He tried to ease out a little so he could get a stroke going but it was not to be. She was too hot, too wet, too tight and he exploded.

"OK," she said patting his back to get off her. She winced again as he withdrew from inside of her. She rolled on her side, turning her back to him and went back to sleep. Floyd looked down at the thin coat of blood and semen on his bare dick and frowned.

"She was a virgin!" he said when it came to him. "Damn, Robinson."

Chapter 7

H ave you ever did some dumb shit and wondered why you did that dumb shit? Well, that's how I felt when I fucked my partner. Especially the night before my boyfriend came home. I woke up that morning feeling just crazy. My head hurt, my stomach hurt and my vagina was sore. The funny part was I really didn't feel guilty. I did it because I wanted to. No, it wasn't right but I wanted so I did it. Yeah it was fucked up but that's not to say I wouldn't do it again.

"You OK?" Floyd asked when they woke up again later that morning. He'd hoped for a replay so he could fuck her properly but she rolled off the bed and found her panties.

"Yeah. Where's my dress?" she asked when a scan of the room didn't reveal it. It showed he had good taste in decor and was neat but she needed her dress. Gerald's plane landed in an hour and she needed her dress.

"In the dryer. I washed it," he said climbing off the bed to retrieve it. Oddly he felt shy when her eyes dropped to his dick and settled there. He pulled his boxer briefs on and headed to get her dress. He returned a moment later. "Hope it didn't shrink."

"Thanks," she said taking the dress from his hand. She lowered it and began to step inside of it.

"You don't want to take a shower? By yourself," he added, throwing his hands up in surrender.

"Nah, I'll shower when I get home. Can you drop me at my car?" she asked.

"Sure, sure. You're parked at the bar. We was both pretty drunk, but you consented. You..." he explained. Her stoic demeanor made him feel slightly guilty so he tried to explain himself.

"We good, yo. We got what we wanted," she said imitating Na-Na since he didn't know her.

"But..." he wondered about the blood. He'd popped enough cherries to know he just popped another. It didn't really compute but he wanted her even more now. Not just to fuck, but to have and to hold.

"Ain't no buts, yo. Now can I catch a ride or I gotta catch a cab?" she shot back. Her acting skills came in handy any time she felt uncomfortable. She could simply morph into another person who was better suited to handle their situation.

"I got something you can ride on," he retorted like his normal self. They bantered like usual as he whipped back over to the bar. The mood got thick when her car came into view. Neither knew how they were supposed to say goodbye so neither did. She hopped out without a word and headed towards her car.

Floyd watched her fat ass until she was in her car. He waited for her to pull away from the curb before leaving himself. He went home to masturbate to her memory while she went to pick up her man.

· · · ·

"HEY BABY! NO, WAIT... Gerald!" Megan practiced on the way out to La-Guardia Airport. She wished she had time to go home and take a shower and change but didn't. She would have to find time to shower and change before they went out to fill the plans they made upon his return. Especially the plan to make love for the first time. A stick a gum helped her breath but did nothing for the semen seeping out of her vagina.

The moment of truth arrived sooner than expected when she saw her chocolate hunk standing on the curb when she reached the concourse. His million dollar smile spread on his handsome face when she pulled up. He rushed around and snatched her from the car just like she did a perp last week.

"Hey, baby. I... ughh," Megan greeted until he gagged her with his tongue. He lifted her off her feet as they made out on the spot.

"Let's get out of here. I have a surprise for you," he said with a wicked grin.

"I um, need to get home so I can shower and change before we go anywhere. I just rolled out of bed!" she said, leaving out whose bed.

"You can do all that when we get where we're going," he insisted. She noticed he changed in an instant while he was way. The old Gerald would suggest and let her decide. This new one just insisted.

"Okaaay," she sang all girly like since he did insist. She followed his directions to a nearby hotel and parked. Guilt gripped her being at what she did just hours ago. "Um...I."

"What? Changed your mind? Since yesterday?" he reminded of her promise to fuck him silly when he came home.

"Huh? No! Come on," she said and unbuckled her seat belt. She beat him out of their car then followed him into the lobby where his room key was waiting. "You don't play!"

"Not about you I don't," he vowed, looking deeply into her eyes. His gaze went through her iris, past her pupils and reached her soul. Guilt made her blink and break off the eye contact. The move registered with Gerald but he was too preoccupied with the issue at hand. He was about to get some pussy.

• • • •

"I HAVE TO TAKE A SHOWER first," Megan pleaded when they entered the room. Gerald had moved on her the moment they entered the room and stuck his tongue back down her throat.

"Want me to come with?" he offered, raising his eyebrows seductively. She did but knew she had to wash Floyd's cum away and that was best done alone.

"No, I'll be out in, a few, minutes," she assured him between kisses on his full lips. She rushed in the bathroom and locked the door behind her. Once the water was at the right temperature, she pulled her dress back off and removed her bra. She shook her head at the crust of dried cum in her panties and decided to wash them as well. When she got under the water she went straight to her sore vagina. "Sss."

Megan stalled until she realized she was stalling and how futile it was. She stepped from the shower and dried herself off. She wrapped her curves in the towel until she realized how futile that too was. It fell to the floor and she stepped back out into the room.

"Damn!" they both muttered when they got a glimpse of the other. She was fine as fuck with the big heavy breast above the rock hard abs. Below that was a fluffy mound of pubic hair concealing a fat vagina.

He was fine as a motherfucker laid out butt naked on the bed. His chiseled chocolate frame was decorated by a thick semi erection laying on his stomach. She approached the bed and climbed on. He moved her hair from her face so he could look at her. Once again her guilt made her cut it short and kiss him.

His dick grew hard as soon as she wrapped her hand around it. She tugged on it vigorously, hoping he would come so they could put this off.

Instead he stopped her and rolled her on her back. He kissed her lips then moved down to her neck. After a brief pit stop, he continued his journey south. Next stop were her firm, ripe titties. He ran circles around her nipples that threatened to make her cum. Then kissed his way down to her inner thighs.

"Wait! You don't have to do that!" she fussed when she realized why he was down there.

"But..." he began, then licked her swollen lips and continued. "I want to."

"Okay," she sang and let him do what he always said he wouldn't do. They often talked about sex even though they hadn't had any. He always said eating pussy was gross but here he was eating pussy. Not just eating it, he was twirling his tongue and doing tricks in the pussy. She still felt the same way about giving head but he could do this any time he wanted.

"Mm-hm," Gerald nodded when an orgasm wracked her body. She writhed line a snake as she came on his tongue. It almost dawned on her to ask how he went from 'eww' about eating pussy, to eating pussy like a pro but this wasn't the time. This was time for the dick. "I'll be gentle."

"Please," she whined since she was already sore from being penetrated. She braced herself and winced as he eased into her body and taking her virginity for the second time. She assumed he would be just as quick as Floyd but he wasn't. They traded kisses as he gently stroked and caressed her. Dick was still too new and uncomfortable for her to reach climax but she loved him inside of her. She felt good enough to admit she was now officially sexually active. She joined the ranks of the fucking.

"Shit, I mean shoot!" he politely corrected as he impolitely bust a nut inside of her. That wasn't part of his plan but it was what happened. It happened twice more before they finally left the room and headed for the Bronx only to get clothes since he booked the room for the weekend.

• • • •

"SUP, YO?" DIANNE ASKED when her granddaughter came in for a pit stop for more clothes the next day. She wasn't sure if she somehow missed her when she came in from celebrating with her partner last night. The same outfit told her she hadn't which means she stayed out all night. She was a grown woman but still. "Where you been, yo?"

"With Gerald," she said when Gerald came in behind her. She couldn't make eye contact with her grandmother but hoped she would leave it alone. She did but only because she didn't get it. She would have never guessed at what really happened though.

"Oh, OK. Hey, sugar! How was California?" she asked and came over to hug the chocolate.

"Great!" he cheered. He couldn't explain how the pretty Cali women turned him out in the six months he was gone. He went for computer training but learned almost every sexual position in the book. Plus two that aren't in any book. The fast women passed the nerdy, pretty man around like candy. They sucked him like candy and taught him how to please a woman.

"Tell her about your trip while I grab some clothes. We're staying in Queens for the weekend," she stated plainly although seeking approval.

"OK, baby." Dianne agreed since again, she was a grown woman. She decided to believe she got the room last night and waited for his plane to land today. That was better than two men in two days like her daughter used to do. She did too once upon a time but this wasn't about her.

"Hey, Paulie," Megan greeted her brother when she entered their shared room. He waved her off and kept talking on the phone. She giggled at his make believe deep voice and knew he was talking to one of the fast little girls around the projects. Grandma was going to be a great grandmother sooner than she thought.

Chapter 8

He loves me Megan thought to herself as Gerald ate her from the back. She felt a little silly with her ass tooted up in the air until he came around and sucked on her vagina. They had been at it all weekend, only stopping for food and fluids.

Gerald used a condom each and every time after that first time. The weekend was a blur of sex and good conversation as they made up for the six months they were apart. Sunday night rolled around quicker than either liked but both had busy weeks ahead of them. This would be their last episode until they found time to hook up again.

Megan came all over his face and collapsed face down on the bed. Gerald rolled a condom on and squeezed inside from behind. She was too sore to enjoy it so she gritted her teeth and took it until he collapsed on her back. She waited for him to catch his breath again before speaking. As much as she loved him and being with him it wasn't what she lived for. She dreamed to be a detective and tomorrow it came true.

"Guess we better get going. Busy day tomorrow," she mentioned and wiggled her hips to signal him to get up.

"Oh, I guess," he groaned and rolled off of her. She spun over so she could see him naked once more. She couldn't get enough of looking at his dark, muscular body. It was a stark contrast from Floyd's beige colored muscles. She thought of that him even while with this him.

They took a last shower together while each entertained separate thoughts. She had a new position and he had applied for one in California. The next time they spoke she was pulling up in front of his building. Neither focused on the goodbye or smack on the lips before he got out. Megan turned up the music on the ride home to drown out her thoughts.

"Honey, I'm home!" Megan sang as she breezed into the apartment. She was just in time for Sunday dinner as well.

"Mmhm," Dianne huffed. She realized her baby was a lady now but that didn't mean she had to accept it quietly. Megan had been gone all weekend with a man. No doubt she was sexually active.

"Aww, is my granny upset?" she teased and kissed her cheeks. Dianne couldn't stay mad and cracked up.

"OK, girl, but I ain't ready to have no great grandchildren running around. You hear me?" Dianne fussed. "Don't be all out it the street like your mother was."

"I, am not, my mother," she said with a haughty aire of indignation.

"Well, even your mother, bad as she is, was still married when she had you!" she reminded. The air went stale for a moment from the terse words. It could continue had Megan wanted but she didn't and changed the subject.

"Where's Claude?" she asked, looking around for her brother. She walked to the window and peered down at the courtyard. "What the... is he smoking?"

"Mmhm. Been smoking menthols with them boys," she sighed. Dianne knew that's how the bad habits start. A cigarette, a beer and next thing you know he's an addict. She opened her mouth to speak but heard the door open and close. "Get his ass!"

Megan hopped down the stairs and burst out of the building. Jax was kicking it with his friends sharing a square when he got popped square in his head.

"What you do that for!" he reeled when he saw who it was. He was ready to fight when he spun around but didn't want to fight his big sister.

"A better question is why you smoking?" she demanded. He opened his mouth to answer but she didn't want one. "Shut up and go upstairs! All y'all go home!"

The eleven and twelve year old boys moaned and groaned but complied. None of them had both parents at home and some had none. It didn't matter because Megan was their mama tonight. She realized she'd been neglecting her baby brother and blamed herself. Of course she wasn't going to tell him that. Instead she vowed to do better.

"You bugging, yo," Jax grumbled behind him as they ascended the pissy stairs.

"Bugging my ass. You like, what nine? And tryna smoke damn stogies!" she shot back almost playfully. Jax heard the mirth in her voice and new he wasn't in that much trouble. "You need to start going to P.A.L."

"I got plenty of pals," he shot back with added bass in his voice. He lost all cool points when he flinched as she spun and faced him in the hallway.

"Look, damn it! I'm not losing you to these damn projects! You will not become a product of this environment." she fussed.

"OK, sheesh," he surrendered. Megan brought it back down and they went inside for Sunday dinner.

• • • •

"UM..." MEGAN HUMMED as she looked through her wardrobe. Most detectives wore business-like attire but she had none. She had sweats, casual jeans and church dresses. Casual jeans were the lesser evil and got the call.

Breakfast was the usual wheat toast and fruit smoothie and she was out the door. Music once again drowned out her thoughts on the ride to work.

"I can't believe I did that," Megan laughed and shook her head at the memory of making love with her partner. Now she had to face the music when she faced him. The moment of truth came the moment she parked her car.

"Yo," Floyd called as Megan stepped out of her car. He'd stepped from his hiding spot where he waited for her arrival. "What's up?"

"With what?" Megan asked seriously. She of course had no idea she fucked the pretty boy's head up. He ignored all his hoes all weekend and sat alone in his apartment thinking of her. Not just the blood or how wet and tight she was, but her. The woman who made him laugh everyday for the last six months. The woman who had his back and he trusted with his life. The woman he fell in love with without knowing. They were like a married couple without the sex, then they had sex.

"Friday? You know, we..." he asked feeling silly. He'd been on the other side of this conversation many a times. Some love struck dame seeking clarity after he put the dick to them. The 'what are we doing' and 'what's our status' talks after he laid some pipe.

"We had a good time. No big deal. We cool. Now let's go to work," she said with a shrug. Floyd frowned at her shifting ass as she walked away. He snapped out of it and followed her into the precinct.

Each detective unit had its own morning briefing just like patrol. The squad's sergeant, Pollack, came in precisely at eight am and got underway.

"Good morning," he began and paused for the greeting to be returned. The man was big on manners and morals which made him the perfect choice for vice. He genuinely wanted to clean up the sordid sex trafficking in the city. "Please welcome our newest additions to the family, Detectives Floyd and Robinson."

"Welcome aboard. Hey, guys. Sup," the men and women of vice murmured. One woman added a curious, "About time."

Megan cocked her head curiously and wondered what she meant by it. The squad of ten was mostly men with Megan being the fourth female. She was also the youngest woman by at least ten years. She was about to get an explanation when the sergeant resumed his briefing.

"We're resuming our operation 'bait and switch' today. Detective Robinson will replace Detective Harper as bait. Be safe out there!" he said leaving Megan wondering what he meant. She was about to find out as the smiling white lady came over.

"Harper," she greeted through her smile and offered her hand. Megan looked at her small hand for a split second before reaching out to shake it.

"Nice to meet you," she said formally even though they saw each other almost daily. The detectives didn't really socialize with beat cops, especially rookies. Kind of like seniors and freshman in high school. They locked eyes and gripped hands like men do. If there's any trace of bitch in a person it will come out during handshake and eye contact. Both women nodded appreciatively when none showed in either.

"Come on. I'll show you the costumes," Harper said leading the way to the shared dressing room. Limited space meant men and women had to share the same space, just not at the same time.

"Costumes?" she asked with a sinking feeling that she would be the bait in the 'bait and switch'. She realized she guessed correctly when they reached the dressing room and Harper reached into a locker.

"What are you? A 7-8?" she asked, hitting the nail on the head. She usually wore a size bigger to compensate for her fat ass.

"Yes, but..." she balked at the tiny shorts she pulled of the gym bag. She was only slightly relieved to see the tags were still on the garments.

"Unless you have your own stuff you want to wear?" the woman asked as if Megan was a thot off duty. She was herself, once upon a time and didn't mean any harm.

"I most certainly do not," Megan shot back and cleared that up. Harper nodded in agreement since she could tell the girl had some scruples about herself. There was a lot of fucking and a lot of gossiping in the precinct and her name was never mentioned. Her partner was a lot, but never hers.

"Well pick your poison. All you have to do is stand on the corner and let the 'Johns' come to you. You'll be wired so make sure you don't offer any services. Let them make the pitch. Do not, get in any, car!" she emphasized to emphasize the danger. "As soon as they say the magic words we'll swoop in and cuff 'em. Got it?"

"Got it!" Megan said enthusiastically.

It wasn't the most glamorous job but it was a start. She locked the door behind Harper when she left and picked out an outfit. Nothing was any better than anything else so she went with her favorite color. The red booty shorts and halter top would look good against her skin tone. She came out of her jeans and squeezed into the shorts. She shook her head at the camel toe in the mirror and turned to check out her booty. It would have looked good if not for the big cotton panties hanging out the bottom. They matched the awkward bra seen under the halter top.

Megan shook her head at what she knew had to be done and did it. She stripped completely naked and put the hoe clothes back on. She scrunched her face up at her nipples showing through the fabric and then the camel toe below. She had to admit she looked sexy but still covered up in a NYPD raincoat hanging on a hook.

"You ready to go?" Detective Hooks asked since he was the lead cop on the detail. Floyd looked relieved when she came out covered up. He still felt it was his duty to protect her just like when they were on patrol.

"I'm ready!" she replied and turned her former partner. "Let's go lock up some bad guys!"

Chapter 9

"Oh my," Megan reeled when she saw all the activity on the block. Females of all colors, shapes, sizes, religions and ethnics backgrounds were present. It was like the United Nations of pussy. Nowhere else on earth could one buy Eskimo, albino and Albanian pussy in one place. Midget pussy, dwarf and amazon pussy. Pussy of all shapes and sizes could be rented for a fee. The term 'selling pussy' is a misnomer since they don't actually get to keep the pussy. They have to give it back the split second after the second they're done.

She couldn't help but notice how young some of the woman looked. Past the whore costumes and beat faces were exploited teens. Young thots who ran away from abusive/or loving homes only to be rented by the nut on the street. She nodded to herself when she vowed to make a dent out here. Just another example of her naivety in thinking she could stop the world's oldest profession. Pussy has always sold better than stocks, drugs and property and it always would.

Her face balled into a snarl when she saw the same young girl who got away from Floyd traipse by in a skirt so short her young ass cheeks were visible. He saw her too but snapped his head away as if he didn't. The girl made her way over to a flashy SUV with rims almost as tall as she was. She paid her new pimp then set off to make him some more money. Her former pimp was serving time but she was scooped up by another before he was finger printed. The colorful pimps strutted around like peacocks in the latest fashions and expensive sneakers. They were all cutthroat competition but socialized mainly to show off their shit. They kicked it like they were cool, waiting for the chance to take each other's hoes and spot. No one ever wants to be number two.

Megan gripped a grudge against the young pimps in an instant. That's who she wanted but today she had to focus on locking up the Johns. They viewed a quick blow job from the passenger seat or back shots in the back seat as harmless but most were married and nothing harms society as much as adultery. It's a crime against God, family and society at the same time. There would be no underage pussy to purchase if there was no demand for it.

"Remember the distress signal," Floyd warned sternly. "You get in trouble just scratch your head with your right hand and I... We're coming!"

"OK," she said warmly. She was touched by his obvious concern even if it made the other cops in the van wonder about their relationship. Most assumed the pretty boy with the rep had bagged and bedded her like all their rest. She actually bagged and bedded him but that was their secret.

"Damn!" all the cops, including Harper gasped when she came out of the raincoat. She stifled a smile at the offhanded compliment and got out the van.

Megan saw thots move and shake her whole life and began to shake as she moved down the block. She was headed to the renegade corner where hoes with no pimps were regulated to. College girls and housewives trying to make ends meet in the meat market. The pimps would sic their hoes on them if they ventured on their turf but also routinely tried to recruit them. It rarely worked since any woman who realized the value of vagina wouldn't part with her pay to some pimp. She barley made it to the corner before cars swerved to pull up on her. There was a near collision as a caddy cut off a Chevy to get to her.

"You working?" the middle aged white man asked through the open window.

"I am at work," Megan replied carefully. She intended to make sure none of her collars got tossed out of court for entrapment.

"How much for some head?" he asked since he couldn't get his dick sucked at home. Truth be told his wife should be arrested right after him. He provided a good life for his wife and kids and couldn't even get any head. That too should be a crime. A class 'A' felony for not sucking dick and sucking dicks only on birthdays and special occasions should be misdemeanor.

"How much are you trying to pay to sodomize me?" she asked specifically and almost blew it. The 'John' frowned at the technical term but a glance at the fat camel toe urged him on like a whisper from Satan himself.

"Is fifty good?" he asked, prepared to double it if need be.

"Yup. Pull around to the parking lot," she said pointing and headed that way. He clapped his hands twice triumphantly and followed directions. Pulled into the parking lot where her backup awaited and got pulled out of his car. A fifty-dollar blow job would cost him many times that when it was all said and done. Bond would be two grand, a hundred and fifty on towing. His name and picture would be on the news, which his wife watched daily and he could lose his job since he wouldn't be back to work. Life would have been so much easier if he could have gotten some head at home.

"One down," Megan said to herself as she sashayed her fine ass back over to her corner. She felt a lot more comfortable from the arrest and it showed in her walked. Floyd frowned as she shook her ass even harder as she went on her way.

By lunch, Megan had set a department record when they recorded their fifteenth arrest. She also caused three accidents as drivers swerved to get to her. That too was another department record. Harper was a nice looking lady but young Megan turned every head including the pimps. It wasn't long before one made his way over to pitch his sales pimping.

"Sup, ma. I see how you bagging them tricks and spitting them out," he said. Every time she left with one she was back in ten or minutes later to get another one. That's four to five dicks an hour and that's good money.

"Cuz this head so hot they cum just bubble out the dick," she said fighting their urge to grimace at the thought.

"Shit, we can make good money together," he said then grimaced to show off the platinum teeth purchased by pussy proceeds.

"We?" she laughed. Floyd frowned at the strange woman talking from inside of Megan. He'd never seen her acting skills and was more confused than anything. "I'm doing good on my own. Fuck I need a pimp for?"

"Cuz I got beans. Any and every kind of pill you need," he said producing and bag of assorted opiates. He was ahead of his time by getting his girls hooked on prescription meds instead of the hard street drugs his peers preferred. The grip was just as strong and less destructive. Crack is hard on the teeth and no one wants a woman to lose a tooth while getting some head.

"You got a number? I'll hit you up later. I'm tryna make my rent today," she asked extending her hand.

"Bet that," he said with a head nod and produced a professional business card.

"Pimpin' Paul. How clever," she said reading the embossed letters. She quickly memorized the number knowing she had to turn the card in. They were hunting tricks today so he would have to wait.

The team broke for lunch after Megan lured the next loser to the parking lot. He was loaded into the paddy wagon and carted off to jail.

"Here!" Floyd grunted and thrust the raincoat at her when she got into the van.

"Thanks. Burgers?" she asked wrapping the coat around her. A couple sets of eyes shot between her legs when she sat down then quickly away. Every man present would have paid for the fat mound of flesh beneath the shorts. Including Floyd who got it for free.

"Better eat light or your stomach will poke out," Harper advised since hers would when she ate her fill.

"I'm 21 years old. My stomach doesn't do that!" she laughed. They headed over to S and S Gourmet Burgers and copped the stuffed burger of the day along with fries. When the returned to work, they pushed the 'bait and switch' arrest record far beyond reach where it still stands to this day.

"Good day, people," Sarge congratulated to all. Everyone knew Megan was the catalyst for the banner day but teamwork required a team.

"You wanna grab dinner or a drink?" Floyd asked. He was mainly hungry but drinks got him inside the woman and ultimately that's where he was trying to be. He avoided and delayed all the chicks that would had been checking for him all day in hopes of spending more time with her.

"Nah, I can't. My boyfriend is home plus I'm supposed to take my brother to the gym. He needs a male figure in his life. I don't want him in the streets," she admitted.

Their time together on patrolled solidified their friendship if nothing else so she didn't mind being candid.

"Where's his dad?" he asked. He knew who her father was since his picture was adorning a wall dedicated to dead cops.

Megan had pushed Jax Senior completely out of her mind until that moment. The scowl that distorted her pretty face told Floyd that this was a touchy subject. Perhaps it was a step dad who touched her or abused her.

"Well let me know if you ever need a hand with him. I wouldn't mind taking him out sometimes," he said honestly. Anything to get next to her again since obviously her so-called man wasn't doing it.

"He would like that. I would like that," she nodded. "Not tonight though cuz we got the gym. Plus my man supposed to take me to eat."

"Plus my man supposed to take me to eat," Floyd mocked to himself as he watched her sweet ass depart. "I wanna take you and eat you!"

Floyd was too frustrated to call one of his lady friends. He couldn't be with the one he wanted and didn't want to be with any of them. He still found himself driving in the same direction they had worked that day. He wasn't quite sure why or what he was doing until he spotted the same young hooker he let get away. He whipped over to the curb and rolled down his window.

"Get in!" he barked and hit the automatic locks. She squinted at him and brought his face into focus.

"You cops stay wanting some free head!" she fussed and got in. "Pull around there."

Floyd followed her directions and parked in a line of cars. It looked like a line of taxis at the airport except for the sex acts going on inside. She leaned over and removed the limp dick from his pants. It stayed limp even after she put it in her mouth. His mind was on Megan despite her working her head.

"Bruh," she complained. She worked by the nut, not the hour but time was still money. She didn't have time to sit there sucking a soft dick.

"My bad," he said minus the remorse and guided her head back down. Two pulls of her pretty lips later and she had a full fledge erection in her mouth. "Mm, that's it Megan. Suck that dick."

The prostitute shook her head while giving him head. She lost control of the situation when he firmly gripped her head with both hands and began to thrust. He gagged her with each thrust as he fucked her face. It didn't last long until he slammed her head down and skeeted directly on her tonsils. It was far too much for her to swallow and cum came out of her mouth and onto his pants. He kept on grinding his hips until he was spent.

"Get the fuck out," he ordered the disposable girl and hit the locks again.

"Hate you fucking cops!" she spat and spit his cum on his leather seats. She was almost dragged when he slammed the car in gear and took off. His frustration was soothed but he still wanted Megan for himself.

Chapter 10

D*ear diary, my grandmother died today. She left everything to me but I don't want none of it. I would rather have her to talk to. Now I only have you, my diary, to talk to. I feel crazy with all this money. First of all, I'm use to working for mine.*

Second of all, a cop looks suspect with a bunch of money. My ass ran out and copped a new BMW, jewelry, furniture, purses and clothes. Not to show off but to get rid of it. I even gave my little sister a thousand dollars when she graduated...

"Oh wow! So... wow!" Megan reeled as the diary revealed the source of the money Officer O'Neil had before she died. She sank into a funk as she remembered the harsh thoughts she harbored about her friend. She decided to visit her grave and apologize first chance she got. In the meanwhile, she put her bright idea in motion and grabbed her phone.

"Pimpin' Paul," Pimpin' Paul said when he answered the unknown number on his phone. A platinum smile spread on his dark lips, assuming it was some new pussy to pander and peddle. He used his customer service tone without a trace of the hard pimping that lay ahead. He was nice and smooth until he bagged a broad then pimped them to death.

"Hey, this... um," Megan paused to come up with a hoe name. She grabbed the first hoe name she knew and said, "Na-Na. We met down on the stroll today?"

"Red shorts? Big titties and fat pussy?" he recalled. He gave his card to several renegade prostitutes but this was the one he was hoping to pull.

"I guess," she sighed. His commodity was cum, so that's what he reduced her to. His was a world of niggas and bitches. Dollars and cents or it didn't make sense. Life is simple for the simple minded.

"So you ready to get with the winning team?" he asked and struck a pose as if she could see him. Not to mention he just liked to strike poses. He had tons of pictures on his social media pages, holding money, hoes and guns. All would one day be used against him in a court of law.

"I'on know. It's either you or a new pimp I met," she said as an idea formed in her mind. "Pimpin' Pretty Boy Floyd is on the set now, so..."

"So what is what! I got the best hoes, best pills. Put you up in a swank apartment and lace you," he said shooting his sales pitch.

"A'ight, let me think about it. I'll hit you up," she said and hung up on his reply. She was too eager to share her bright idea with Floyd to hear what he had to say.

"Yo..." Floyd answered, trying to sound nonchalant when he took Megan's call. This was the first time she called since they hooked up. Before it wasn't uncommon for either to call the other off duty to finish a conversation or debate from earlier in the day.

"Ooh ooh! I got an idea! Check it!" she said bouncing around the living room. "OK, so I called that pimp guy from earlier and..."

"And how and why?" he cut in and asked since she turned the card in and no one told her to do anything else.

"Um..." she replied to that question and moved on. "So look, you pose as a pimp. I'll be your whore, bottom bitch, thank you very much and we can infiltrate the scene. Gather enough evidence to shut the whole shit down! No more buying and selling women and girls."

"Bruh..." he said shaking his head. "First of all, we'll never shut the sex trade down. There are junior pimps and hoes waiting in the wings for their shot at the big leagues. And second, did you ask Sarge?"

"No," she said and he could hear her pout through the line. She was disappointed that he wasn't with her program. They skirted a rule or two in the past to make arrests and made detective as a result.

"I mean it sounds like a good idea but we ain't been in vice but a couple days. Let's try to not get fired already." he sighed.

"You wack," was all she had and hung up. Her next call was to Gerald to see where he was. Another glance at the clock showed he was late for their late night date.

"Shush," Gerald warned to the woman on top of him. The next door neighbor had been chasing the old him for years. The new him came back and gave her what she was after.

"Mm, OK," she agreed as she rode him. She busied her tongue on his Adam's apple to mute her moans.

"Hello. What's up, bae?" he asked as if he wasn't standing her up for the next chick.

"What's up is you supposed to be here. Eating me," she added with a wicked grin. Her vagina throbbed and moistened when it heard her.

"Um yeah, I... shit, got caught up. Couldn't leave cuz um," he said as she squeezed and rocked on his cock.

"Are you jacking off cuz you couldn't get over here to me?" she said giving him a way out.

"Uh yeah," he decided, thrusting upwards into his neighbor. She clamped down on his neck and rode him faster.

"You gonna cum for me?" she dared and slipped a hand into her panties. She thought they were engaged in another of their phone sex sessions but he was fucking the lady next door.

"Shit! Mm, argh!" he grunted and filled his condom up. "I gotta go!"

"I... well damn," she said when the line went dead in her ear. She abandoned her vagina and got up to go to her room. A frown adorned her face from his odd behavior.

• • • •

"GOOD MORNING," SARGE greeted to get the morning briefing underway. "Detective Floyd came to me an idea to pose as a pimp and infiltrate the pimping scene."

"What the..." Megan snapped and snapped her head in his direction.

"Sarge, she came up with it," he clarified, pointing at Megan. Her face softened in an instant.

"I wouldn't care if Santa Claus dropped the idea down the chimney, it's a good idea for the team and the team will make it happen! Now, Floyd will transform into a pimp, Robinson and Williams will be his ladies of the night," he explained and went on to expound the rest of the plan.

Pimps, dope boys and niggas in general love to brag. They love to tell all their business and show off. Once it was all on tape they would all be indicted, arrested and convicted. The rest of the morning was logistics and planning. They adjourned for the day with the plans to meet up later for their first night of the new operation.

"Wanna grab a bite?" Floyd asked as they left the building. He expected her to decline and say something about her man but she didn't.

"Bet," she agreed since she was hungry and Gerald would be at work. They had eaten lunch together every day when they shared a patrol car. That was before he ate her and everything changed. "I'll follow you."

Floyd wanted to drive straight to his apartment since she was supposed to be following him. Lunch would be a good old fashion 69 with back shots for desert. Instead they went to S and S chicken and waffles and got a table. He ordered the jerk fried chicken and buttermilk waffles while she went with ranch fried and red velvet waffles.

"You'll make a good pimp!" Megan tossed to break the awkward silence. Floyd had to process the mouth full of food before he could reply. He held up a finger while he chewed, swallowed and washed it down with his drink.

"How you figure? Cuz a lot of women throw themselves at me? I'm their bad guy cuz I'm handsome? I'll have you know I would be the perfect husband and father! It's my fault chicks want me just for my looks? That's some real bull-shit!"

"Take a breath, bruh. I was just thinking you're a good cop and can pull it off," she explained. "Why you so sensitive lately?"

"Because," he replied and that's all she was getting. No way was he telling her he was in love with her. He twisted his lips as she raved about her boyfriend again just like when they shared a patrol car.

• • • •

"PIMPING FLOYD, I PRESUME?" Megan laughed when she arrived back at the office and saw Floyd.

"Ya know it!" she sang in her hoe voice. Floyd was amazed at how effortlessly she could slip in and out of character. She was too at times and was beginning to wonder which her was really her.

All men present pretended to be busy when she and Williams slipped into the dressing room to get into character. Wanda Williams was a pretty, brown, mid thirties bombshell in her own right but Megan was a fine, young stallion. They were all disappointed when Megan came out bundled up in the raincoat once again. Williams almost made up for it in bright yellow booty shorts and wife beater.

"Our ride for the night," Floyd said holding up a key with a large L on it. He pressed the fob and a shiny Lexus hollered back.

"Is that..." Megan laughed when she recognized the vehicle as the same one the pimp they arrested drove. The city confiscated it for the drugs and put it back in service. Wanda stepped in front of Megan to claim the front seat. Her seniority prevented Megan from complaining. She stuck her tongue out at the back of her head and hopped in behind her.

Floyd parked the flashy car with the other flashy cars and got out. The moment of truth came when Megan got out and came out of the raincoat. She had on a tiny black dress with absolutely nothing underneath. A perfect impression of her round nipples could clearly be seen through the thin fabric.

"Fuck!" Floyd heard himself exclaim. Megan heard it too and giggled out loud.

"You like this type of shit, huh?" she dared and turned to the side so he could see her ass jetting out from her slim waist. She wobbled in the high heels but caught herself on the car.

"Not on you I don't," he admitted proudly. He would rather see her in a wedding dress but wasn't going to tell her that. "Let's get it!"

"You two go together?" Wanda asked to end the speculation and curiosity. She too heard about the pretty boy's rep and wanted to tap that herself.

"No!" they both shot back so quickly she nodded in agreement. Floyd just got himself some ass and didn't know it yet. He extended both elbows to escort his hoes into the joint.

Megan gladly put her arm his arm as they headed towards the bar. Not only would it make the right impression when they entered but it would keep her from falling on her pretty ass.

"So I said bitch, get my... damn!" Pimpin' Paul exclaimed mid sentence as the couple walked in. The light from outside shined through her dress putting her fluffy muff on display.

"Who that?" Pimp-Z asked checking them both out as they headed to the bar.

"New nigga. Pimpin' Floyd," he bragged since he knew. "He look like he getting to the money. All iced out and shit."

"I bet. Look at the bitch on his arm!" Zaddeous said in awe. Megan couldn't climb up on the bar stool so she stood by Floyd's side with all that ass on display. Technically there were two but they only focused on one.

"Let me go holla at this nigga," Paul announced and stood. He sashayed his way over in full pimp regalia looking like a sailboat in blue and white stripes.

"Here he comes," Megan informed through clenched teeth when she seen him approach.

"You must be Pimpin' Floyd. I heard a lot about you," Paul lied and extended his diamond and platinum laced fingers.

"Word," Floyd replied slapping him five instead of a handshake. "This Na-Na and Sugar."

"We met," he shot back hoping to make it sound like more than it was. "I know you new around here but we got protocols. One is common courtesy if a pimp wanna take a spin in one of your bitches. Pick one of mines cuz I need to take this one for a ride."

"I am new around here so let me get my feet planted. This here pussy cost money. It's so good I pay for it my damn self. I take my money out of one pocket and put it in the other. Best pussy on the planet!" He vowed. Megan couldn't help but blush and smile at the compliment. She knew that wasn't part of the act from his tone. She didn't get to revel in it for long before he ordered her to hit the street. "Go get 'em, girl."

"OK, daddy," she purred. He leaned in for a kiss and palmed her ass. She gritted her teeth but let him put his tongue in her mouth. They both felt her knees buckle before she spun and rushed from the bar. She didn't have any panties on which meant no panty liner. Fucking with him would have juice running down to her ankles.

Wanda waited her turn and kissed him just like he kissed Megan. Except she let her hand rest on his dick. She pulled back and gave him a look that invited him to some ass. He watched both asses as they left the bar.

Both partners had productive nights posing as pimp and hoe. She steered twenty more men to the paddy wagon while he gleamed a ton of information from the talkative pimps. He sprang for rounds of drinks while they took turns telling all their business.

Chapter 11

"**G**ood job tonight," Megan said patting her little brother on his head. He ducked and knocked her hand away just she expected. She started off training him how to avoid getting hit and he obviously got it.

"Chill! My waves!" he fussed and smoothed them back down. Neither of them knew how much of his father's traits he picked up through DNA alone. The older he got the more he looked like his father but Megan's memory of the man had faded. She could clearly identify the traits they both shared from their mutual mother. "Is Gerald still coming to get me this weekend?"

"I don't know? I mean, I guess." she guessed since he'd kept her guessing since he came home. He seemed so different, so distant. Floyd offered to take her little brother out for guy time but that was her man's job. She'd pressed him on the weeks since he came back but nothing came of it yet.

What she didn't know was that he was wide open now since getting turned out, out west. She was so wrapped up at work that she hardly noticed they rarely spoke. They made their cases against Paul, Zaddeous and four more pimps for pimping, pandering, money laundering and a host of drug charges. The hoe stroll paused for a whole half an hour before more pimps and hoes filled the void. The demand of tricks meant there would always be a supply of hoes to treat them.

"Well, I'm going to bed," Jax announced as soon as they stepped into the apartment. One thing about their workouts, he went right to sleep at night.

"Um, how about you take a shower first?" she frowned up since they shared a room. "You smell like a young ram and talking about going to bed!"

"Oh," he replied. He was still at the age where he didn't care whether he bathed or not.

"Boys," Dianne huffed from her perch on the sofa. Now that her babies were home she could go to bed herself. "Is Gerald coming?"

Megan pressed her lips together tightly to prevent smiling at her inside joke. She knew Gerald would definitely be coming if he came over. The moment passed when she wondered if he was coming over or not.

"He's supposed to," she said and heard herself whine. Her grandmother heard it too and lifted her head from her crocheting with a concerned frown.

She knew that first love usually isn't the one that lasts but it's that last love that lasts forever.

"Is everything OK with you two?" she dared with a weary frown.

"I guess? I mean, we both be busy... " she said making excuses for him. She decided to call and see for herself.

"Hey, um, hey. Sup?" Gerald greeted guiltily when he took the call. Only loyalty made him answer since he had company.

"You busy?" was the obvious question since he sure sounded busy. He was about to get busy with yet another woman. Once the cat's out the bag it's damn near impossible to get it back inside.

"Who me? Nah, I'm not doing nothing," he lied. The woman realized he was talking to his woman and went for his zipper. There are a lot of challenges out there but the 'talk to your woman while getting your dick sucked' trumps them all. "Mmhm, nothinnnn at all."

"So, you still coming over?" she asked trying to sound sexy as one can with their grandmother looking at them.

"Ummm, I mmm, can't. Work tomorrow. I'll hit you up," he said and hung up on her when it got too intense. He winced as he watched the pretty Puerto Rican woman work. A blow job is work and she was putting in overtime.

"OK, oh I understand. So I'll catch you tomorrow. Mmhm. OK, bye. Love you too," she said since she had an audience. She was a great actress but grandma didn't buy tickets to her show.

"You OK?" she asked furrowing her brow at the phony display.

"Girl, I'm fine. About to take my shower and go to bed." she said and went to do just that.

Jax showered in five minutes flat and went to bed. Megan attempted to catch a nut but caught feelings instead. She scrubbed angrily and got out of the tub. She half ass dried off her ass and got dressed in sweats, sneakers and her service weapon. She snuck out of the apartment and rode across town to Gerald's building. She found a spot behind a little chick car and parked. She felt a little silly and decided to go home and go to bed. No sooner did the thought process did Gerald step from his building. He cast a protective glance up and down the block. She froze when his gaze ran right over her but he didn't see her. A woman stepped out behind him and took his hand. She was still frozen when they turned and headed straight for her. The car in front of her chirped and un-locked when the woman hit the remote.

"You gonna call me, papi?" the woman asked when they reached her car and leaned against it.

"You know I am," he assured her and leaned down to kiss her. Megan heard her heart break when they made out furiously just feet from her. "A'ight, you gone fuck around and its gonna be round five! Right here on the sidewalk!"

"Bring it!" she dared and grabbed his dick through his pants.

"Tomorrow, mama. I'll holla," he declined and stepped back. They shared a peck as she got in and started the car. Gerald smiled and waved until she pulled off. He turned his head and came face to face with Megan. "Yo!"

Megan saw all that needed to be said and slammed her car in gear. He had to hop out the way to avoid getting his feet run over. He rushed back inside to call her but she didn't answer. She vowed to never answer his call again. She sped all the way home and parked.

"Sup, Megan," the stick up kids greeted as she stomped through the projects. She mumbled a reply and kept on moving. A second thought stopped her in her tracks and spread a smile on her face.

"Yo, remember my boyfriend?" she asked and waited for the to reply in the affirmative. "Well his ghetto pass is revoked. It's whatever next time he come through here."

"Say no more," they assured her. It wasn't the first time they had been sicced on an ex. Probably wouldn't be the last either. Break up with a project chick and never come back. She may invite you for closure and get a closed casket. These dudes weren't killers but they would rob anyone, anywhere, especially here.

It was late but Megan was too restless for sleep. She didn't have any girlfriends to beat their ears up so she called the next best thing. The closest thing she had to a friend.

"Excuse me," Floyd said when he saw the name, number and picture on his phone. He had taken a picture of Megan's profile when she wasn't looking and made it her caller id. "Sup, you OK?"

"I guess," she sighed. "You wasn't sleeping was you?"

"Sleep, at... 2 am? Nah," he said making a joke out of the truth.

"Yeah, it is late. I ain't want nothing," she said and hung up. O'Neil's words from the diary came back, 'an undercover cop can't have man.'

"You good?" Wanda asked when Floyd came back to bed.

"Yes," he replied even though he wondered what she wanted. Megan called to kick it before but never this late.

"Well..." she replied and spread her thick thighs. "Since we both up."

Floyd took the invitation and rolled on top of her. He grew an erection quickly as they traded kisses. She reached down and guided him inside of her hot box and squeezed. He tucked his face into the crook of her neck and threw that dick. A few minutes later he snatched out and bust on her stomach.

"You ain't had to do that. I ain't one of these young broads about to get pregnant on you," she reminded. He grunted a reply and rolled off to go to sleep. They all had to work in the morning.

• • • •

MEGAN FELT CRAZY WHEN she awoke the next morning. Part of it was lack of sleep but there was something else she couldn't quite put her finger on. She knew her grandmother was up cooking and hoped breakfast would ease her queasy stomach.

"Morning, guys. I'll... " she began until the smells of biscuits and beef bacon overwhelmed her. She tried to fight the salty taste in her mouth, then took off towards the bath room. She just made it to the toilet before the content of her stomach erupted from her mouth. She tried to stand but found she wasn't quite done. She heaved a few more times until finally finished. After rinsing her mouth and brushing her teeth she returned to the kitchen as if nothing happened. "Morning, guys!"

"Morning," Jax greeted through a mouthful of morning cereal. Nothing phased him except the latest games so he thought nothing of the incident. Not grandma though.

"A-yo, what you got going on, B?" she asked getting real hood on her. She tried to be a sweet old lady most of the time but being in the hood means sometimes the hood comes out.

"What you mean?" Megan asked. It was genuine since she didn't know what that bout was about herself. "My stomach jacked up. Must be something I ate?"

"Mmhm," Dianne dared with her head cocked and lips twisted. "I'll talk to you when you get home!"

"OK, whatever," she shrugged and ate her toast. The dry bread soothed her jumpy stomach enough to drink some juice. She just ignored her grandmother's gaze as she ate.

"I got your whatever," she assured her before she left for work.

Megan arrived at work early as usual and waited for briefing. Wanda was waiting for her and slid next to her as soon as she sat down.

"Good morning. Everything OK?" Megan asked curiously of the curious move. They were coworkers, not friends so she wondered what she wanted.

"Yeah, I just wanted you to hear it from me first. Me and Floyd are together now. I see y'all close and all but we doing our thing and I need you to respect it," she laid out.

"Bruh, me and Floyd are cool. Friends even because we were partners. I don't have nothing to do with his personal life," she assured her with a face to match her tone.

"Oh, cuz you had called last night why we was tryna fuck so..." she added and watched for a reaction. She got one but not the one she was looking for.

"Man I called him cuz we cool. Nothing more. You can have him cuz I don't want him!" she shot back.

"Good morning, ladies," Floyd greeted as he came in and headed to the coffee jar. He turned curiously when no reply came.

"Good morning," Wanda sang seductively while Megan snarled at him. He shook his head and took his usual seat. Wanda got up and took her seat and waited for briefing.

The sergeant laid out the squad's next mission to crack a child porn ring. The girls ran from 15 to 16 instead of 5 and 6 but it was child pornography nonetheless. Floyd felt the heat and wondered why Megan was glaring at the side of his head.

He would have to wait until after work to find out what was on her mind. Wanda stuck to his side like a Siamese side chick so Megan shot him a text message.

'Follow me. I have something to show you' it read and spread a curious frown on his face.

"Everything OK?" Wanda asked seeing his reaction and trying to peep at his screen. "We still on for dinner right?"

"Uh, yeah, sure. I have to make a quick run out to..." he explained but stopped short since he didn't know where she was leading him. "I'll call you when I get in."

He didn't hear her reply since Megan had already left the office. He rushed out to see her pulling out of her parking spot. He ran to his car and tore out after her. He caught the tail end of her car as it turned the corner. It took a few blocks for him to catch up. He made eye contact with her through her mirror and called her phone.

'Nope' she mouthed in the mirror and shook her head.

"Queens?" he asked when she jumped on the expressway. Little did he know the only hotel she ever knew of was the one Gerald took her to when he came home. He was even more confused when she pulled up to the office and went inside. She came out a few minutes later and dangled a key.

"You coming?" she asked but didn't wait for an answer. She knew the answer anyway and made her way to the room. He was right behind her when she walked inside.

"Why are we here? What you supposed to be showing me?" he asked. She replied with a wicked grin and peeled off her jeans. The ass cheeks protruding from the French cut panties gave him an instant erection. The shirt went over her head and off came the bra. Her firm breast barely moved when they came out. She finally stepped out of her panties and climbed on the bed. She crossed her arms on the pillow and laid on her head while her ass went up in the air. Her plump vagina popped out let a present, presented to Floyd to enjoy.

"Think I won't!" he cheered and came in behind her. Her body jumped when he flicked his tongue on the hot box. He leaned back to watch it blossom and bloom. Soon it was swollen and glistening as he stripped down to his own birthday suit.

"Eat it like you love me," she chuckled. The joke was on her since he did love her and that's exactly how he ate her. He had her young ass howling through orgasm after orgasm. She tried to run after the first one but he flipped on her stomach and licked her to another one.

"Please fuck me!" she pleaded after the third one rocked her world. Floyd's face was wet with her juices as he stood. He rolled a condom on his throbbing erection and gave himself a few strokes.

"You can have, whatever, you, shit!... want," he assured her as he worked his way inside of her. He planned to fuck the daylights out of her to make up for last time. It sounded like a good idea but it wasn't to be. The good, young pussy was too wet, too hot and too tight. Combined with her pretty fuck face, it was too much. "Argh! Mmm, shit! Whew!"

"I know, right!" she laughed as fuck faces contorted his handsome features. "Get up. I gotta get home,"

"Now?" he reeled. He was ready for dinner. A movie, marriage or whatever. Anything but going home.

"Yeah, my grandmother need to talk to me about something," she recalled. "Oh and you can thank your smart mouth woman for getting you some pussy."

"What? Who?" he asked. He certainly would thank whoever helped him get inside of her once again.

"Wanda Williams. Bitch stepped to me this morning talking shit. I just want her to know I can have you whenever I want," she said in her ghetto girl persona. She dressed and left while he was stammering and explaining.

"You can though," he said to himself. "You can..."

Chapter 12

I really can't believe some of the situations I get myself into. I swear being smart don't mean shit sometimes.

First my ass sleep with two dudes in the same day and here I go again. Got my legs cocked up with the next man just working away. I don't even know dudes name....

"Go to bed, Jax!" Dianne demanded in her no nonsense tone when Megan stepped into the apartment.

"Bed? It's still light outside!" he pleaded. "I'm not five."

"Well, go outside and play. And you better not come back in her smelling like menthols and malt liquor!" she fussed.

Oh Lord, she on one today, Megan thought and shook her head.

"I'll give you something to shake your head about!" she fussed like an ass whipping was imminent. They both knew it wasn't since she never had to whip her as a child so she certainly wouldn't be whipping her as a grown woman.

"What did I do grandma?" she sighed and plopped down next to her on the sofa. She frowned down at the small box Dianne extended to her. She could read just fine but still asked, "What's that?"

"It's a 'you spending nights out with a man and now throwing up in the morning test'. Take it in the bathroom, pee on it and bring it back, right back," the grandmother explained.

"I ain't even late and I used a condom and I..." she grumbled as she stood and stomped to the bathroom. She wasn't late but she wasn't particularly regular either. She realized she was slightly sore from the quick, but recent sex when she sat on the toilet. She was relieved she had to pee anyway and got a good flow going instantly. She wiped herself and the test strip before washing her hands and stepping back out. "Hmp."

"Mmhm," Dianne said accepting the test. She flipped her wrist to check the time then backed it up with a glance at the clock on the wall. The five minutes passed in silence except Megan blowing her breath in mock exasperation. The moment of truth came and Dianne checked the strip. She let out a sigh and stood. She tossed the test on Megan's lap and walked to her room.

"Nuh uh!" Megan fussed at the positive test. She shook her head, then the test but it didn't change. She was still fully dressed so she stood and rushed out of the apartment.

"Sup, Megan! Where you going?" Jax asked so he could ride. Any other time she would have invited him along but today she just ignored him. She rushed around the corner to the supermarket and rushed inside. There were several brands of pregnancy test at various prices on the shelf.

"No wonder!" she cheered when she saw her grandmother bought the cheapest one. She triumphantly grabbed the two most expensive test and marched over to the counter. She drove confidently back to the projects and went upstairs. She was relieved her grandmother was still in her room so she could take the test and hit her with a 'how you like me now' and toss the negative test at her.

"But how? She asked after the first positive test then broke down and cried when she checked the second one. She sank down to the tile and wept like a baby. Sorrow turned to anger when she remembered Gerald with the Puerto Rican mami. He knocked her up and cheated on her. She stood to ride uptown and beat him up. Then she recalled sleeping with Floyd just hours before. It dawned on her that she didn't know which one actually knocked her up. The weight of the revelation sank her back down to the floor.

"Yo, I gotta use the bathroom!" Jax proclaimed, doing the 'I gotta pee' dance while knocking on the door.

Megan wanted to fuss him out but a glance at her watch showed she'd been in there for over an hour.

"So use it," she quipped as she opened the door and walked out. She headed straight down the hall and knocked on Dianne's door.

"Come in, baby," she called out calmly since she had calmed down. This wasn't what she wanted for her granddaughter but you don't always get what you want. Everything has already been written. All that's left to do is live it.

"Hey, grandma. I'm sorry," she sighed and sat down on her bed. "I'm not keeping it. It was an accident and I'm not ready to be a single mom."

"Why single? What's up with Gerald?" Dianne asked and leaned up to hear the reply. Had she been a mind reader she would have been shocked to read about Floyd.

"He never came back from California. I don't know who they sent back," she said shaking her head. She decided to never shed a tear over him or any other man, ever. Her daddy got all her tears, so fuck these dudes.

"Well, I hope you learned a lesson from all this mess. Men change. He loves you, but men change," she tried to explain. Her brow furrowed as she realized men are just as complicated as women. Sometimes more.

"I did. I have," she vowed and stood. She learned not to have sex with more than one man a day, use condoms and put herself first.

• • • •

"WHAT HAPPENED TO YOU last night?" Wanda demanded, putting her hand on her shapely hip when Floyd arrived at work. His mind flashed to holding those same hips while hitting her from behind. He literally shook his head to clear the thought from his mind.

"A better question is what did you tell Robinson? About us?" he insisted.

"Nothing. Said we together now is all. Why? Thought you guys were just partners," she dared and eased up so he could kiss her if he wanted. She glanced at the clock to see if there was time to fuck him in the dressing room before briefing.

"We are just friends. Just like me and you," he said stepping back. He turned his back and walked over to his desk. She shrugged her shoulders and wrote him off too.

"Good morning!" Megan greeted loudly and held up a bag from the bakery. "I bought bagels!"

Wanda twisted her lips at Megan and her bagels. She decided she wasn't fucking with either of them. She watched her closely to see if she was the reason Floyd took his good loving away. Oddly she didn't treat him any different than the other detectives. He was obviously sweating her but she didn't give him the time of day.

Floyd stared at Megan's head during the briefing. Luckily there wouldn't be a quiz because he didn't hear a word the sergeant said. Megan waited 'til end of the briefing and pushed up on the boss.

"Quick word, Sarge?" she asked when she got him alone. He answered with his face and she went on. "I got a medical thing. I'll need a day or two."

"You OK?" he asked peering at her to see if he could see anything wrong with her. "We're close to shutting down the child porn operations."

"Wait for me boss. A day, two tops." she assured him. He gave his blessing with a nod and she was off to handle her business.

Megan hated leaving the action for even a day or two but this had to be done and soon as possible. Floyd watched her curiously as she left the precinct. She only knew of one place up in the Bronx so she headed back uptown.

After finding a parking spot she got buzzed into the clinic. She made a bee-line to the counter and confirmed her appointment.

"Officer Robinson," she said using the title that got her a quick appointment in the busy clinic.

"Mmhm," the woman said as she entered her in the computer. "Have a seat. You'll be called when a room is available."

Megan nodded, turned and came face to face with Yvonne. She usually ducked the girls from home when away from home but had no time.

"Sup, yo. What you doing here?" she asked even though there was really only one reason one comes to an abortion clinic.

"Um, I um...Shit this nigga done knocked my ass up. Told the nigga don't buss in me and... " she said, going into her ghetto girl persona. She usually channeled Na-Na when needed but used a combination of them all when at home.

"Man, me too!" Yvonne replied. She already had five at home so she opted for a third abortion. The pill or condoms would be easier and cheaper but she was irresponsible and he liked his pussy raw dog. They sat down and chatted until Megan was called to the back.

"In here," a nurse directed. She followed her in and recorded her vital signs. "Disrobe and the doctor will be in in a minute."

Minutes around there take twenty to tick off and finally the doctor came in. He moved with assembly line like efficiency. Mainly because the high volume clinic sucked unwanted children out of women and girls from open to close.

Megan craned her neck trying to look at the stranger looking at her vagina. She shook her head at showing that much of herself without even getting his name.

She was suddenly too shy to ask so she entertained herself by making up names for him. The pass time passed enough time to get her through the procedure.

"All set," the doctor announced when she was no longer pregnant. He removed his gloves on his way out to kill the next kid.

"You have a ride, right?" the nurse asked as Megan sat up. She had to repeat herself to break the deep thought trance she was in.

"Huh? Oh, nah. I drove," she said and stood. She wobbled slightly and steadied herself on the table.

"Um, not. Just call someone or a taxi," the woman advised. Na-Na once rode a bike home from an abortion but she was a vet. Megan called a taxi and went home.

• • • •

"YOU OK?" DIANNE ASKED when Megan came in looking frazzled.

"Mmhm," she said with a head nod on her way down the hall. She entered her room and plopped on her bed. She was more mentally tired than physically and practically passed out.

Megan dreamt about her phone ringing nonstop until her ringing phone woke her up. She saw Gerald's number and turned the phone completely off. She went back to sleep for a few hours until she heard her grandmother fussing in the front room.

"What now?" she grumbled and got up. She used the hall wall to get to the living room where Dianne was giving Gerald the business.

"You had a good girl. Not one of these... oh hey, baby. Why you up?" she asked.

"Let me talk to him," Megan groaned and sat down of the sofa.

"OK, baby," she said and sat down beside her, glaring up at him. There was an awkward silence as they sat there looking at each other. "Oh! You mean alone. OK, but I'll be in my room if you need me."

"Well... " Megan began but stopped when she heard her grandmother's steps stop. The old lady sucked her teeth and continued down the hall so Megan resumed. "I ain't even mad at you. We've gone in different directions so..."

"Wait, so you call yourself breaking up with me? Me?" he reiterated pointing at himself to be sure. Getting a lot of pussy can go to a man's head literally and figuratively.

"Yeah, you!" she laughed at his arrogance. "So kick rocks before I call Dianne back out here."

"Fuck you, Dianne, and um whatever your little brother's name is... " he ranted on the way out. Megan intended to walk him out safely since his ghetto pass had been revoked. Now she just posted up in the window to watch the action.

Megan seen the stickup kids debating on whether or not he was bait or not. One reminded them that Megan lifted her protection and they sprang into action. Gerald tried to run but got tracked down, beat up and relieved of his property. He walked barefoot and shirtless to the train and Megan went back to bed.

Chapter 13

The next year and a half was a blur. We made a ton of arrest and got a bunch of pedophiles and pimps off the street. Floyd was right about one thing cuz as soon as we locked one up another one takes their place. It was literally pimps and hoes on deck. Speaking of Floyd, I fucked him a few times. Whenever I felt like it mainly but especially anytime he got a so-called girlfriend. Life was good and then it got better. Then that woman came back.

"Good morning," the sergeant greeted to start the morning briefing. "Great job yesterday, people. That lowlife pimp who pimped the little girls was sentenced to a hundred and twenty years."

"He got off easy if you ask me," Wanda said even though no one did ask her. She was still right since this creep had a houseful of children he pimped out to pedophiles. They got a bunch of them too but there were plenty more out there.

"Well, yeah," the sergeant agreed and nodded. "We have some good news and bad news. Good news is Robinson has been reassigned to narcotics. Bad news is Robinson has been reassigned to narcotics. Not just narcotics but the city wide narcotics task force!"

"I,did? I did!" Megan popped up and shouted. Everyone clapped and cheered except for Floyd. Not just because she got promoted before he did but also because she was leaving him. He just could not figure the woman out. One minute she's distant, then in his bed the next. She kept him so off balance he couldn't even keep a girlfriend.

"You did! Congratulations," he said joining the applause. Once the cheers died down he continued his briefing so Megan could complete her last day on the vice squad.

"I'll ride with you," Megan offered when he set out to investigate a legal massage parlor offering illegal happy endings. He shrugged so she fell in line behind him. They rode in virtual silence except the silly men and women on the morning show. Megan laughed along with them but Floyd's jaw was tight.

"You're not happy for me?" she whined. She would never admit it but he was her best friend if not her only friend.

"Huh? Yeah! Of course I am! Why would you ask me that?" he reeled. He was slightly in his feelings until hearing it out loud. He had a few years seniority on her so it stung that she made it before he did. Little did he know she was requested.

"Oh, OK. Cuz I was about to say," she huffed and puffed. "So you not me out to celebrate?"

"I would if I could. Me and Amy getting kinda serious so... " he lied. He caught on to her antics and played it to his advantage.

"Well, if she's your woman she should understand you're a cop and your partner comes first! I wish I would let some man tell me... "

"OK, OK. Let's go out for drinks. After work, couple drinks but that's it," he said sternly.

" OK, couple drinks. That's it," she repeated but she didn't even drink. She had some good vagina juice for him to drink though. "So anyway, what we gonna do with Sunshine massage parlor?"

"I'll pose as a customer and see what's not on the menu," he shrugged.

"You wired?" she asked. Quite a few of their best cases were made as a result of wiretaps.

"Not yet. I need to peep the operations first," he replied as the GPS announced the arrival.

"OK, just don't have no happy ending!" she joked although very serious. She had a happy ending for him when they got off work.

"Bruh..." he said, twisting his lips into a 'yeah right'. "I am a cop."

"True, my bad. I'll be right here," she apologized. She watched his booty as he walked away just like he did hers. Once he disappeared into the building she recorded the surrounding area on a camera.

"Welcome to Sunshine massage!" an elderly Oriental woman greeted with a bow. She came across as a sweet old lady but Iceburg Slim had nothing on her pimping.

"Thanks. I saw your ad online. I printed the coupon," he said presenting the coupon. She saw the code that meant he viewed their page on the adult sites. The regular site had a different code.

"My granddaughter, Susie, will take care of you," she said with a knowing nod.

She used the intercom to summon Susie. Floyd kept a poker face but wondered if they weren't barking up the wrong tree. Surely she wasn't pimping her own granddaughter. Little did he know she pimped her daughters, nieces, and cousins. If they had a vagina she was renting it out.

"Hello," a pretty, yet pretty young woman with unusually large breast greeted as she came out. She smiled at him and did a curtsy to her. She was 19 but could pass for 14 when she needed to. The woman said something in their language. Whatever it meant made her shoot a quick glance down at his crotch.

"Hey," he greeted and paid the standard fare for a standard massage. She extended her small hand and led him to the back. They entered a small room with a massage table.

"Take all clothes off," she instructed in broken English even though she spoke perfect English. While disrobed she readied her oils and equipment. Floyd was glad he didn't wear a wire since there was nowhere to hide it. He laid his slacks and shirt on the chair and pulled his undershirt off. She let her robe drop and reveal a firm young, yellow body underneath. "Underwear too."

"Um, OK." he said and stepped out of his boxers.

She nodded at his bobbing semi erection as if greeting it. He climbed on the table face down and got a pretty good standard massage. He was almost ready for a nap before she ordered him to flip.

Susie worked his shoulders and chest, making sure her firm breast rubbed his body. As expected his dick throbbed erect. She worked around it, brushing against it and getting him worked up. He finally had enough and placed her small hand on his thick dick.

"Extra," she said and gave it a few tugs before pulling away. She wrapped her breast around his shaft and explained once more. "Extra."

"Ok. My wallet in pants," he said in her brand of broken English. She retrieved his wallet and handed it to him while she pulled out a credit card reader.

"Fifty or one hundred?" she asked before she swiped. He pondered for second since he just paid rent. Plus he had a date for later so he opted for the discounted happy ending.

"Fifty," he decided since it was his personal money. Had it been on the city's dime he would have gotten the deluxe service.

She swiped the card and paused. It beeped when approved causing her to smile and nod. She climbed on top of Floyd and wrapped his dick into her cleavage.

"Mmm," he moaned from the sensual sensation. It only got better when she popped him into her small mouth. Her vagina was even tighter than that but he wouldn't find out for fifty bucks. He didn't realized how backed up he was until he exploded in her mouth.

"Mph!" she mentioned as her mouth filled with salty semen. She stroked the shaft and milked him dry. Once he was spent she rolled off and spit into the garbage pail. Obviously swallowing was extra too. Like super sized or something. "You come back?"

"I come back!" he nodded enthusiastically. He left out the part about search warrants and handcuffs. He liked blow jobs as much as the next man but he was still a cop after all.

"So?" Megan asked when he returned. He was feeling nice and relaxed as he slid into the passenger seat since she had changed places.

"They offered extra services for extra pay. The girl had a card reader and everything," he revealed. She had some dynamite head but he concealed that part of it.

"Did you get some?" she laughed even though she felt a tinge of jealousy and held her breath. She would never admit it but she hated whenever he started seeing someone new. She wanted him all to herself even if she didn't want him. She just didn't want anyone else to have him. An undercover cop can't have a man anyway.

"Come on, yo!" he shot back indignantly. She smiled internally and pulled off. She finished her last day in vice and met up with Floyd after work to celebrate.

• • • •

"I'M COMING!" MEGAN shouted with her legs straight up in the air. Floyd twirled his tongue inside of her and shoved her over the edge. She gripped handfuls of his sheets and busted a nut in his mouth. He clamped his lips on hers and drank from the tap.

"My turn?" he asked hopefully as he flipped on his back with his erection in hand.

"If, I, sucked dick, I would, definitely, suck this," she said rubbing her face on his dick. "But, I don't!"

"Ha ha," he replied to her chuckles. He watched her as she rolled a condom down and carefully check the tip. She vowed to never have another abortion, no matter what or who. The best way to protect that vow was to not get pregnant.

"Did, this thing, get, bigger?" she asked as she wriggled the head inside of her. She shook her head at his cocky smile as she slowly slid down his shaft. That wiped the smile off his face when that hot, tight vagina gripped his dick. He could feel her juices run down and pool on the bed beneath him.

"Did you get tighter?" he asked and grabbed her ass. He worked her hips up and down while thrusting upwards into her. He smiled again when her face contorted with pleasure. He picked up his pace when she moaned from an impending orgasm.

"Shit!" she fussed and came all over his dick.

He flipped her over onto her back without pulling out and kept on pumping and humping. Getting off earlier in the day kept him rock hard. They both knew this was their last time together since she was transferring to the task force. He fucked her like it was his last time too. Several hours and several orgasms later they huddled up in orgasmic shivers. No one said a word since neither knew which words to say. They were both in love but neither would admit it. Megan finally rolled off his bed and stood. She couldn't bare to look at him so she dressed and left without saying goodbye.

"Why you crying, yo!" Megan demanded to her reflection in her rearview mirror. She felt something running down her face and glanced up to see what it was. She was shocked by the tears and quickly wiped them away. "We don't cry over no dudes!"

Megan avoided the courtyard since she didn't want to kick it. She entered the building by the front and headed up the stairs. She took a second to compose herself before opening the door. She plastered a phony smile on her face, stepped inside and came face to face with her mother.

Chapter 14

"What the... " Megan began until a terse head shake from her grandmother caught the 'fuck' in her throat. Jax sat on the chair looking angry with his arms crossed. "Thought you had another year or two?"

"If you read the letters I sent, I told you they granted me parole," Michelle said smoothing her waves down with her hand. She was lucky Megan didn't read the letter stating how the parole board gave her some play since her daughter was a cop. She would have definitely intervened against her coming back there.

"Yeah, well," was all the explanation she had for her. Megan took in her appearance and decided, "So what, you a stud now?"

"Something like that but I know how to keep my business, my business." she replied.

"I can't tell cuz when you was on..." Megan began with a dry chuckle but Dianne shut that down too.

"Look you two! We family. Family don't turn their backs on family," she offered hopefully. "Your mom just did a bid. She's a new woman!"

"Sure they turn their back on family. She did," she shot back. "Come on, Stephan. Let's go!"

Jax stood to leave with his sister then stopped. He rushed over and unhooked his game system from the TV and carried it to the back with him. He planned to sleep with it under his pillow that night and every night until she was gone. Even he realized she wouldn't be there long.

"Them some rude kids," Michelle fussed and shook her head. This wasn't the warm welcome she expected. She just knew her children would slam into her and hug her to the ground when they saw her. Then again Michelle was out of her mind.

"Well, you did abandon them a few times to smoke drugs and go to jail so..." her mother tossed back at her. "So you was really in their eating them girls out? You gone keep doing it or get yourself a man?"

"Men don't have pussy so I won't be getting no man," she said getting a kick out making her mother uncomfortable.

"How long you staying out this time?" she asked to keep the volley going.

"I ain't going back to dope or prison!" she assured her. She was sure about the latter but she could hear her name being called from way off in the distance. Her drug habit just festered in prison since she didn't get help. Doing time just hit the pause button so it was just a matter of time.

"Well don't end up like Reese either. They found her froze to death on the roof with a crack pipe in her mouth. They had to wait 'til she thawed out to remove it," Dianne relayed and managed not to laugh this time because that was some funny shit. It was just deserts for the damage she did the house on Long Island.

"I ain't going out like that either. Trust me. I'll make it this time," Michelle nodded. They both hoped it was true because neither had it in them to go through all that again.

"Why she gotta come back here?" Jax griped when he and his sister reached their room. She pressed her lips together tightly to keep from laughing at him putting the game system under his pillow.

"I'on know. Hopefully she won't be here long. If she do, I'm moving out," she vowed, actually considering it for the first time. She was a grown woman still sharing a bedroom with her little brother but didn't want to leave.

"I'm coming with you!" he vowed and hopped to his feet ready to leave. "Can grandma come too? Just let that lady have this apartment."

"That's not a bad idea. We good. She won't be around long. She never is," Megan said.

She got her change of clothes and went to wash the recent sex from her body. Tomorrow was a new day and she made it to narcotics.

• • • •

"GOOD MORNING. I MADE breakfast!" Michelle cheered when her children emerged from the rear. "I used to do all the cooking in the joint. Mainly cuz I can cook but also cuz I don't be eating everyone food. Some of them chicks be nasty."

"Come on, Leroy. I'll buy you breakfast," Megan said and steered her little brother out of the apartment. Michelle wanted to cry but didn't know how. Instead she got mad like most lonely people. She would have logged onto social media and made some angry post like most lonely people but didn't have an account. She did have a few bucks though and planned to go get a drink.

"You gotta give them some time, baby. You been gone for a long time. Don't push," Dianne comforted. She wanted nothing more than her whole family living together in harmony. She wanted it just as bad people in hell wanted ice water. Neither was going to get what they wanted.

"Shit, I left my game!" Jax remembered as they entered the deli. He was set to turn around and go get it but his big sister stopped him.

"Chill, Pablo. She cool for now," she nodded. She figured they would be okay until she started smoking again. Megan splurged on calories and ordered pastrami and eggs with cheese on Kaiser rolls for them both. She wanted to stay and eat with him but wanted to be early, not just on time for her first day.

"I love you," Jax blurted and threw his arms around his sister and squeezed.

"It's just pastrami," she replied feeling awkward from the sudden affection. She had gone so long without any it felt strange. He broke off the hug and darted across the street. She watched him blend into the throngs of kids before heading over to the garage for her car.

The GPS guided her to the new address in a nondescript building. She parked next to some nondescript cars and went inside. She understood the magnitude of her new assignment when greeted by an armed, uniformed officer.

"Detective Robinson," she said handing him her badge. She stifled a proud smile anytime she said or heard the words 'Detective Robinson.'

"Detective Robinson," he acknowledged with a nod and handed it back. He leaned out to watch her ass as she entered the secure location. He wasn't privy to the operations going on inside but did notice they had some fine women cops working it, especially that new Puerto Rican sergeant.

Megan was in awe how they retrofitted the old building into a modern command center. She could hear the whirling of computers and servers as she walked by a control room. She followed the signs to the large briefing room that resembled a college classroom. As usual she was early but so was everyone else. The front rows were taken so she found one several rows back and took a seat. The low din of muted chatter came to a sudden halt when the suits entered.

"Good morning. My name is Special Agent Mark Hernandez with the FBI. This is Major James from the New York City police department. We are in command of a new federal and local task force against drugs and organized crime..." he announced. He paused to let the gravity of the heavy words to sink in.

The co-chiefs of the task force took turns laying out the problems and the agenda. Local police would make cases for the feds to prosecute. No more slaps on the wrist, the Feds knock blocks off. Megan scanned the room as they spoke and noticed all the women were pretty. Nothing less than a dime which meant she had to be one too. Her head shook as O'Neil's words came to her mind. She, along with the other women, were bait. She wanted to stand up and walk out but didn't. Couldn't, wouldn't, so she stayed.

"Please meet the five sergeants who will direct the five sub teams," Major James said as four men and one woman walked into the room. Megan blinked, rubbed her eyes and blinked some more. Nothing changed and it was still her academy roommate, Marisol Ruiz. Sergeant Ruiz that is now.

"How the..." she began to say but again the 'fuck' got caught in her throat when her name was called. She let out a sigh when she was assigned to Ruiz's team. Little did she know it was Ruiz who requested her. She remembered their talks at night and knew she wanted to be a good cop. Not to mention, she was fine.

The meeting adjourned and the groups of twenty separated into their separate units. Besides Megan there was a very pretty, very dark detective named Carlita Carmichael and a sexy white one named Amber Johansen. Name tags on desk directed everyone to their places as Marisol stood front and center.

"Well hello, everyone," Marisol greeted and paused while it was returned. Even Megan greeted cheerfully even though she was still on the fence about this assignment. She didn't have time for games when she could just go back to Floyd and vice.

"We are assigned to the Bronx and Westchester counties. Our first target is a drug crew out of the Sound View projects. They are moving large amounts of cocaine, marijuana and now opiates... " she explained while the slide show flipped on the screen.

Blah, blah, blah Megan thought to herself as she listened. Shit, her own projects had a booming drug trade. She knew who slung what and who they all got work from. A smile spread on her face since she knew it was time to put them out of business. She was powerless when they were running trains on her mother for drugs but there was plenty she would do now. Now she was narcotics and would serve her projects up on a silver platter

"The crew is run by Rico Hawkins... " she explained as the pretty boy splashed on the screen. Megan straightened up in her chair and caught Marisol's attention. "Did you have something to add, Detective Robinson?"

"Um, no," she lied. She remembered him from the double date with her cousin years ago when she was in high school.

"He's pretty, but pretty dangerous as well. Reports say he recently murdered his right hand man, Walter Woods," she said as her half of the double date appeared with a click of the remote. "He allegedly killed him so he could sleep with his girlfriend. We have an apartment in place in the projects. Robinson and Carmichael will move in and pose as college students. New meat is sure to get Rico's attention. Get 'em girls!"

Chapter 15

"Why can't I come?" Jax whined, pouted and stomped as Megan packed. His woeful tone gave her pause to consider it, then shook her head 'no' since it just wasn't possible.

"Bruh, I already told you it's for my job. I'm not leaving you. I'm never leaving you!" she stressed.

"OK," he relented since she'd never lied to him yet. She never called him by his right name but hadn't lied to him either. He looked up to his big sister as big brother, mother and father. He was the main reason she was still here.

Megan let out a frustrated sigh as she packed her clothes for the assignment. Most of them were plain Jane and none of them could pass for project thots. She heard her own project thots burst out in laughter and went over to the window. Most times their laughter was to get attention from the dope boys instead of something actually being funny. Na-Na and them held the bench down during the day but the next generation of baby mamas had the night shift. Megan's head nodded to what they had on and she knew a shopping trip was in her near future.

"Wanna take a ride over to Fordham road with me?" she asked needlessly since she knew he wouldn't say no.

"You gonna buy me a game?" he dared as if the answer mattered. He was riding weather she said yes or no.

"I might," she replied with a crooked smile that meant he was getting a new game. They both put their sneakers and headed for the front. Both tensed knowing that woman would be in the living room.

"Hey, Megan and Jax. Where you guys heading?" Michelle tried again when they emerged. She tried everyday and everyday got a quick answer in passing.

"Out," Megan said pulling her brother through the door. Michelle snarled at her daughter as she departed but kept her remarks to herself.

"Gotta give them time," Dianne reminded from the kitchen even though it had been over a week. She recalled Megan not talking to her brother until he was over four years old, so she didn't say how much time.

"I ain't got much time," she mumbled to herself and rocked. Her t-cell count dropped by the day and her days were numbered. Her mother came out of the kitchen just in time to see the door close behind her. She marched straight over to the dope boy bench and copped some dope.

Michelle was high as a kite by the time her children reached the iconic shopping district. She copped crack while Jax got the latest game and Megan bought booty shorts and halter tops since that's what Na-Na and them wore on a regular despite the wrinkles of childbirth and C-sections.

• • • •

"WHERE SHE AT?" MEGAN asked when she came in and saw her mother's spot was empty. She surprised herself when she heard the concern in her voice. Everyone wants to have a mother and she was no exception, except no one wants to have a mother like that.

"Gone," Dianne said with a sad sigh. She watched her daughter head straight to the dope boys and buy dope. She knew she would come back but she was gone in the figurative sense.

"Good!" Jax fussed and rushed down the hall to make sure his game was still there. They both watched him until he was gone before speaking.

"She went to the bench?" Megan asked expecting a yes but hoping for a no.

"Like she was shot out of a cannon," Dianne said, shaking her head. "There's something you should know. Why they paroled her early."

"I know, cuz she told them people 'oh my daughter is a cop' and they gave her some play," she replied.

"Probably but that's not it. Your mother is sick."

"In her head! I don't know if it's the dope or what but she gone! I seen her talking to a potato! She..."

"Is dying. She got full blown AIDS. Weeks, a month maybe," Dianne cut in before she would say things she would regret.

"But she... don't look sick? She ain't skinny or nothing," Megan pleaded. There was nothing her grandmother could say so she said nothing. They both sat there in silence for hours until it was past both of their bedtimes.

Megan peeped out her window once she got into bed. She twisted her lips seeing her mother walking away from the night shift dope boys.

"She got a fat ass!" one cheered. These teens were still pushing Tonka trucks and big wheels when she went to prison. She was new meat to dudes who just developed a taste blow jobs and back shots.

Megan shook her head once more and laid down. She had a busy day ahead of her and needed some sleep.

• • • •

"HERE WE GO!" DETECTIVE Carmichael said as she parked the undercover Jetta in the projects parking lot. "Remember, my name is Jazzy. Do not call me Carlita."

"I can't call you Detective Carmichael either?" Megan asked with wide eye wonder. She was beginning to take a dislike for her already since she kept treating her like she was slow. She was the ranking officer in the field since she had a few years on her but Megan wasn't slow by any means.

"No, Nay-Nay. Don't call me detective either," she huffed.

"That's Na-Na. Worry about you getting my name right. Now can we please go make a case on these clowns?" she asked indignantly.

Carmichael didn't respond but she did lead the way into the building that would be their new home until they built a case on Rico. Drugs were fine but they wanted him on the bodies as well.

"A-yo! Sup, chocolate! Light skin!" the dope boys called from their bench. Every projects has dope boys and all dope boys have a bench. Both women lifted their heads and twisted their hips as they ignored the catcalls. If they started fucking at the bottom they would never reach the top. If the pussy was deemed exclusive or elusive, its stock would go higher and Rico would hear about it.

"Hole up. Who y'all be?" a teen asked as he caught up and caught Megan by her arm.

"I be that chick that slaps niggas for grabbing on they arm!" Megan shot back in full Na-Na mode. Carmichael furrowed her brow and snapped her head in her direction to see who spoke.

"My bad, ma!" he surrendered and raised his hands. "I was just tryna welcome you to the hood. Here."

"Good looking," Megan said accepting the blunt he handed to her. She turned and thanked him again with a marvelous display of ass as she walked away.

The women rode the elevator up to the top floor and found their end unit. Just like Megan's back home it had a view of two sides of the projects. They could keep tabs on the courtyard as well as Rico's apartment directly across from them.

"That wasn't bad out there. You might be alright," she said. It wasn't much of a compliment so Megan didn't reply. Instead she pulled out an evidence bag and receipt. "Um, what are you doing?"

"Booking it into evidence?" Megan shot back curiously. It was drugs so she didn't know what else to do with it.

"How 'bout not," Carmichael quipped and took it from her. She walked into the kitchen and turned the stove on. The gas range clicked until it caught and produced a blue flame. She pulled her long hair out of her face and leaned in to light it.

Megan watched her take a few tokes just to see if she was really going to smoke it. She did and passed it to her. Megan declined and went to the window to watch the action. By the time her partner was high, she ascertained who were the lieutenants, muscle and which building held the stash.

• • • •

THE GIRLS' COVER INCLUDED college so they had time for briefing and debriefing as well as personal stuff. Megan took advantage of the couple hours down time by checking on her brother. Her first stop was the ATM for cash.

"Megan!" Jax cheered and abandoned his friends when his big sister came into the courtyard. She threw her arms open and he ran straight into them.

"What's up, Huey. You good, yo?" she asked and peered down at him to check for herself.

"I'm good. She don't be in the apartment," he said as if trying to comfort her angst. "When you coming home?"

"Soon," she replied since she didn't know. It had been a couple of days and they rarely saw Rico. Meanwhile Carmichael traded numbers with a couple of dope boys. They offered to come through and smoke and she accepted.

Megan saw her mother cut between buildings and went after her. She walked briskly and caught up with her before she entered the next building.

"Yo, m, m, shit, ma!" she called after some work. The word got stuck in her mouth until she remembered her plight.

"Me? What!" Michelle reeled in mock shock and pointed at herself.

"Yeah, ma. Look, I just wanted to make sure you good. Here..." she said, thrusting some cash at her. "It's two hundred bucks. That should last right?"

"I might can stretch it but why you giving me money? What your grandmother told you?" she pouted.

"Nothing!" she lied. She was such a good actor her mother believed it and softened. Truth be told she wanted to make sure she didn't have to trick with the dope boys who would who spread it to the young thots who inherited the bench from Na-Na and them. Secondly, she wanted to make sure her last days were comfortable. A fucked up hood version of hospice care. Instead of morphine she would have crack cocaine.

* * * *

"WHO!" MEGAN CALLED out through the door as Carmichael put away the binoculars. She gave a thumbs up and she opened the door. She walked away and took a seat on the sofa.

"Sup, yo. This Doo-doo," Charles introduced as he and his friend stepped inside. Carmichael invited him over and he brought a friend for a friend.

"Sup, Doo-doo. This Na-Na," she said, hooking a thumb as Megan sat on the sofa with school books on her lap.

"Sup," he nodded at her big thighs under the books. She nodded back and pretended to read.

"Smoke one!" Charles cheered and produced a blunt. Doo-doo held up a bag with his and a forty ounce malt liquor. "Y'all got glasses?"

"Hole up," Carmichael said and went to get some. She was back in a flash as the lighter flashed to light the blunt. Doo-doo made a big deal out of producing one of his own, handing it to Megan since she was supposed to be his.

"I'm good, yo. I gotta study for school," she said causing Carmichael to snap her head at her. She tried to shoot her one of those looks a mom gives her child out in public instead of cursing them out.

"Tuh," Megan huffed since she wasn't her child. She pretended to study but the only notes she took were the ones from the guys telling them all they knew about everything, hoping to impress them enough to fuck them.

"'Member when Carlos shot Frankie?" Doo-doo asked across the room to Charles.

"Only cuz he shot him first. He just shot Po-boy last night in front of the bodega!" he said putting several charges on the man. They went back and forth, dry snitching on the entire neighborhood but avoided Rico's name. Once the weed and beer were depleted he got around to what he came for. "Let me talk you alone."

"OK," Carmichael agreed and stood. She took him into her room by his hand and closed the door behind them.

"Which room is yours?" Doo-doo asked since he was ready to fuck as well.

"Come on," Megan said to his delight and stood. He followed her shifting hips as she led the way and opened the door.

"Huh?" he asked when it was the front door, leading to the hallway.

"I have to study," she said politely nudging him out.

"Damn dike!" he decided as he marched down the hall. That could be the only reason she didn't want to get with him. He was Doo-doo after all.

Megan couldn't believe the sounds of sex coming from Carmichael's room. She frowned up, wondering why she was having sex with the underling. He was cute and all but once word got around that they were some jump offs they would never get next to Rico. Word was already spreading that she was gay as soon as Doo-doo reached the bench.

An hour later, a very happy Charles emerged from the room. She stepped out behind him with her hair all over her head.

"Where Doo-doo go?" he asked, looking around. Megan fought against the sarcastic remark on the tip of her tongue.

"I can only tell you where he didn't go," she shot back instead of saying Doo-doo goes in the toilet like she wanted to. Carmichael slobbed him down once more at the door and let him out. She spun and she and Megan had words.

"What the hell is wrong with you!" they both shouted at each other. "Me? You! I'm telling Sarge!"

Chapter 16

"**S**up, youngins. Who wanna credit me a couple rocks 'til in the morning?" Michelle asked confidently when she reached the bench. The question was answered with utter silence since no one wanted to do it. "Y'all lil niggas deaf or something? Front me some dope!"

"No can do, ma. It's a violation of rule number six," one finally spoke up.

"Rule number six?" she asked cocking her head in confusion. She scratched her scalp to help her think, plus it itched.

"Rule number six, that got damn credit, dead it. Think a crack head paying you back, forget it!" he rapped the Notorious B.I.G classic while another played beat box with his mouth. The grown kids got a good laugh out of their standard reply when someone ask for credit.

"Just suck some dick like err one else?" another shrugged like it was a simple solution. And it was. Wars have started and ended behind some good ass head. Helen of Troy wasn't just pretty, that head game was ridiculous.

"How 'bout I give y'all some of this good hot pussy instead? I'll take all y'all up to the roof and break you off." she dared. They got a good laugh at her expense but she who laughed last had full blown AIDS.

"Bet!" the rapper said, taking her up on the challenge. Two stayed behind to man the trap while two more followed her into the building. No one wanted to walk up all those stairs so they waited on the elevator.

"Bitch got a fat ass!" one said while fondling her on their ride up to the roof. The other one reached over and copped a feel as if to confirm. Michelle turned to let him palm her ass as well. The door open to the top floor and they all got out. They walked up one flight to the rooftop motel.

"Who first?" Michelle asked as she stepped out of her shorts and laid on the gravel below.

"Me!" the rapper said and dropped his pants. He kneeled between her legs and slipped inside of her. "Shit tight, yo!"

"I ain't, mmm, had, none, in a ssss, while," she hissed as it got good to her. She liked pussy just fine when it was the only thing available, but she still loved her some dick. "Mm, get it, youngin. Dig it out! Get it!"

He did get it and thrusted to her coaching. She busted a nut just before he did and got up. The next teen dove in and began humping while the other went to get the others. The four of them took two turns a piece inside the infected vagina. These projects were about to be as hot as Chernobyl.

• • • •

"OK, OK. ONE AT A TIME," Marisol cut in as the two women began fussing at once. She called them both into her office after briefing to settle their dispute.

"Go 'head," Megan dared since she felt she was in the right. She would let her tell her side of the story then shut it down with her own.

"No, you go! You don't tell me what to do!" Carmichael shot back, pulling rank. "See, that's the problem. She think she runs me."

"Well I run you both so, Robinson, you tell me what's going on. Then your team leader can tell me hers," Marisol demanded. She may have fucked her way up the ladder but that didn't mean she couldn't handle the job. She displayed a willingness to do whatever it took to close cases and at the end of the day that's all that really matters.

"Well, we're meeting all the low level dealers, 'go-fors' and 'do boys'. Got some good Intel on base operations, info on a couple of assaults," Megan began.

"That's great! That's exactly what you're supposed to be doing so you can get next to Rico," Marisol cut in.

"Except she keep fucking the help. We ain't never gonna get anywhere near Rico if he thinks we're some thots," she added making their bosses head nod. Marisol turned to face Carmichael for her side of the story.

"We're supposed to be college girls. 'Sposed to turn up and have fun, but your girl here won't smoke, won't drink, and won't give the guys any play. Shit, they think she gay!" she fussed, pointing at Megan.

"I see. OK then. Give us a minute, Carlita," Marisol said softly. She waited until she left and the door closed behind her before speaking. "Look, no one can tell you to use drugs or have sex. No one can be mad if you don't."

"Thank you!" Megan shot back but didn't quite get where she was going with it.

"Some detectives do whatever... it takes to make a case and you can't be mad at them either. I remember how hungry you was in the academy. That's why I selected you but maybe this assignment isn't for you. If you don't want to do whatever's needed then maybe you can go back to vice and... "

"No!" Megan shouted and surprised them both. These were the same words from O'Neil's diary, doubting if she could handle the work. "I can do it. My thing is she's tainted now. Rico ain't tryna fuck with the same chicks his underlings fucked. What baller you know wanna fuck behind his help? They be wanting exclusive booty. Chicks no one else hit. Well, at least no one they know."

"You right," Marisol nodded. She certainly dealt with enough ballers to know.

"Let her keep doing her thing and you keep doing you. College kids smoke weed, drink and turn up."

"I understand," she said with an inward sigh. She had no intentions on letting anyone inside of her but knew she had to give a little as well.

"Let them keep thinking you gay though. That may be your ticket in!" Marisol nodded.

• • • •

MEGAN STOPPED AT THE ATM once again before she headed uptown to the Bronx. She shook her head to erase the thought of wondering when Michelle would kick the bucket so she wouldn't have to keep spending so much money. She planned to give her a hundred dollars a day so she wouldn't have to trick or steal. It was a good plan except for the fact that Michelle smoked three hundred dollars a day.

She saw a heavy police presence in the projects when she arrived telling her something happened. It came as no surprise since this was the projects and shit happens. She parked sideways and rushed out to make sure whatever shit that happened didn't happen to her brother or grandmother.

"What happened?" she demanded flashing her badge to paramedics pushing a stretcher with someone stretched out on it.

"GSW to the torso. Another one upstairs DOA." he said in passing. She looked around and saw her brother in the crowd made a beeline to him. "Upstairs!"

"OK. I ain't shoot him! Dang!" he fussed as she herded him into the building.

"Where's... ma?" Megan asked when she and Jax entered the apartment. Her grandmother had been watching the action from the window and turned.

"I'on know?" she shrugged like Jax would do. It seemed like he was rubbing off on her more and more as of late.

"Y'all stay put. Let me see what's going on?" she said trying to sound official. She even hung her detective badge around her neck but really she was just being nosey. She found a detective and inquired. "What we got?"

"We?" he asked raising his eyebrows. He saw her badge but it didn't make her a 'we' since she didn't work in his precinct. "You in the 44th?"

"Nah, I live here. Grew up here. Probably know all the players," she said and got his attention.

"Andrew Foye, age 19, took two in his side. Nick Hansen, dead from a shot to back of his head. Baggies, scales and residue suggest it was drug related," he revealed. Megan revealed nothing since she planned to present everything she had to the task force.

"Lil Drew and Niko. I know them from around the projects," she shrugged and walked away. The detective raised his palms like what the fuck when she departed without helping.

"Yo, what happened?" she asked when she reached Na-Na and the gang. They just looked at her like she had three heads and stayed quiet. Megan looked down at herself and saw the problem. She tucked her badge into her shirt and asked again. "What happened, yo?"

"Lil Drew and Niko went renegade. They started getting they work from the Dominicans instead of Nasty," Na-Na began. Everyone likes to be in on some good gossip so Yvonne took it from there.

"Nasty told them they can't sell in the projects if they wasn't buying from him. They said 'fuck him' and he fucked them," she explained.

The girls gossiped like they did everyday but this wasn't like any other day. Today a cop was sitting and taking notes.

Megan found her mother in the crowd and broke her off with her hospice fund. She looked near death but the cocaine in her system kept her on her feet. She may have been dead already and just moving from the large amount of drugs she consumed. She broke off the awkward silence by turning and leaving without saying goodbye.

••••

"SUP, YO," MEGAN GREETED as she and Carmichael met up to go to their home in the projects. They were down with their classes for the day and it was time to turn up.

"Sup with you? Ruiz said you down with the program," she replied and raised an eyebrow.

"Some of it. I mean I'll loosen up, a little. I'm not fucking though. Pussy is worth more before a nigga get it," she said quoting her grandmother when she told her about the birds and the bees. It was crass but true.

"Whatever. Just don't be no stick in the mud... whatever that means," she said and cracked them both up. The good laugh loosened the tension and they looked like happy friends by the time the reached Sound View projects.

"I eat pussy too! You ain't gotta get no chick to do it!" a man from the bench called out. The other men got a kick out of it and laughed along with him except Doo-doo that is who looked hurt. Charles got to report how good the new pussy was while he got dissed. The laughter came to a sudden halt when a man emerged from a building. The platinum and diamond jewelry glistened in the sunlight almost obscuring his face. Megan recognized him immediately as Rico. He locked eyes with her as Doo-doo and Charles filled him in on who they were.

Megan hoped she didn't fuck up by not revealing how she knew the man when he cocked his head and squinting at her. He didn't recognize her but his curiosity was sparked by the sexy lesbian.

"Yo, who those bitches?" Rico said zooming in on the light skin one. He acknowledged the sexy chocolate chick but preferred yellow.

"I smashed the black one," Charles proudly proclaimed. He turned to Doo-doo to fill him in about the other.

"She gay," he nodded to make it true. True or false it meant new pussy that niggas weren't jumping up and down in and that caught his attention.

"Where they stay?" he asked even though they entered building 18.

"18," he replied just as Megan stepped inside and came face to face with her grandmother.

Megan let out a horrified gasp but Mrs. Mahatma looked straight ahead and didn't acknowledge her. She didn't even recognize her since she never looked at her as a child nor any of the pictures Rohan use to give her.

"What's wrong with you?" Carmichael asked when her face went from yellow to white.

"Huh? Oh, nothing. Nothing at all," she lied. The snub hurt her feelings just as much now as when she was a child.

Chapter 17

"**W**ho?" Megan shouted at the door when she walked over to answer it. In her mind she asked 'which one of these thirsty niggas here to fuck my thirsty ass partner'. She determined Carmichael was really a sheltered, suburban hoe who liked dealing with street dudes. She peeped through the peephole and reeled back.

"Who is it?" Carmichael asked in a tone that matched Megan's shocked reaction.

"Rico," she whispered as he replied on the other side of the. She regained her composure and gave herself a quick once over. Her big nipples could be seen just fine through the shirt so she hiked her shorts up into her crotch and opened the door.

"Hello?" she asked, twisting up her face. She was glad she answered to give him attitude because Carmichael probably would have dropped and sucked his dick on the spot.

"My name is Rico. These are my projects so I wanted to come meet my new tenants. I been hearing about you two," he said and stepped forward.

"What, you from the housing authority?" Megan shot back and looked him up and down like she wasn't impressed.

"You must be Na-Na and she's Jazzy?," he guessed correctly since Megan wasn't buying what he was selling but Carmichael spread her legs enough for him to see under her skirt.

"Come in," Carmichael invited and patted the sofa next to her. "You got weed?"

"I got weed," he replied, nodding as he took a seat. He tossed a bag containing an ounce of colorful, fluffy weed. "Roll up."

Megan shook her head internally as she watched Carmichael putting on a show as she rolled the blunt. Rico watched too as she seductively licked and sucked the cigar. She was just supposed to moisten it enough to split but almost made it come in her mouth.

"What school y'all go to?" he asked turning his attention back to Megan.

"N.Y.U. It's too expensive to stay downtown so we found this spot," she explained as rehearsed. She made sure they strictly stuck to the agreed upon cover story.

"And you don't like dudes?" he asked bluntly. She was super fine up close and he would wife her up if he could. Her diking meant no one was dicking and that's an attractive feature in a woman.

"I like dudes for for what they good for. Fixing cars and cutting the grass," she said quite believably.

"I like guys!" Carmichael shouted and bounced to get the attention back to her.

"I heard," Rico said without turning to face her. She lit the freshly rolled blunt as he gave Megan the third degree. She kept a remarkable balance of flirty and standoffish that made him want her even more. Carmichael tried to pass him the blunt but he leaned back so Megan could get it.

The moment of truth and they both knew it. Carmichael watched smugly waiting for her to choke, literally and go into a coughing fit. To her surprise Megan took an expert pull and held the smoke. She and Rico resumed conversation as she took two tokes and passed.

"Check, I'm having a little function at my crib this weekend. Why don't you fall through?" he invited.

"Here in Sound view?" Megan asked. She had watched his movements enough to know he didn't live here. He showed his face daily but laid his head elsewhere at night. They wanted to put a tracking device on any one of the many cars he showed up in but couldn't even get close.

"Nah, I got another spot. Put your number in," he ordered and handed her his phone. She followed directions and put her undercover number in. She began to hand it back but stopped and pulled it back. She turned it around and aimed it at the plump mound between her legs and clicked a picture. "Since you kept looking."

• • • •

MICHELLE YAWNED DEEPLY as a young dope boy dug deep inside of her. She probably would have enjoyed his dick slinging if she hadn't been so tired. His steady pounding was the only thing keeping her awake at the moment.

Oh shit! oh shit! oh..shit! he fussed and bust a nut inside of her. He was pretty sure the older crack head wouldn't get pregnant like his teenage girlfriend. They were currently on their third child at the moment. She was down on the bench with one in a stroller and the other running around while she smoked weed.

Break me off! Michelle demanded and reached her palm behind her before he even pulled out of her. Back in the day she could have clamped that tight box down and prevented him from leaving. Now the floppy vagina had no walls or grip and couldn't even keep a tampon in place.

I got you ma. he said and pulled a few rocks from his pocket. He put his dick away and joined the other dope boys in the front room.

Nasty decided to move the sales indoors until the heat of the murder cooled off some. It shouldn't take long since someone was always getting themselves killed. Lil Drew survived the shooting but wasn't telling who shot him. He got the message loud and clear and planned to join the team once again as soon as he got out of ICU.

The whole projects knew about it but no one was talking. Not to police anyway but they talked amongst themselves just plenty. Megan was one of them so she was able to get the whole scoop. She planned to make a case against Nasty and the whole crew as soon as they wrapped up with Rico.

Thanks sugar. she said graciously and accepted her pay. She let out a yawn even deeper than the last and pulled out her pipe. Gonna' take me a blast and take my ass to bed!

Michelle's eyes went as wide as dinner plates as she sucked the sizzling drugs into her body. She actually felt a piece of her soul slip out as the drugs coursed through her. She sucked the rock to oblivion but didn't get any higher. She tried another rock but still didn't get where she was tryin' to go. She did feel a little more of her soul rise from her body.

Oh well, she shrugged as she accepted defeat and stood. This wasn't the first time she had burned herself out and couldn't get high. She decided to go to her mothers house to crash for a day or two.

You leaving? a teen asked as she staggered through the living room. He was hoping to take another spin inside her before she left.

Yeah. I'll see you fellows tomorrow, she said and let herself out. Another yawn racked her frail frame to its core. She had to jean against the wall just to get down the hall.

Michelle felt bogged down as if walking through quicksand as she crossed the courtyard. She barely made it to her building for needing to stop for another rest. It took all she had to pull the metal door open and enter the stairwell.

I need a break, she announced and took a seat on the steps. She leaned against the cinder block wall and let out a yawn. She yawned again, blinked then died right there on the spot. A low gurgling from her throat signaled the departure of her sordid soul from the abused body.

Again? Jax sighed and shook his head when he came across her the next morning on his way to school. It wasn't his first time seeing her asleep in the stairs. He stepped over her just like he always did and went along his way.

A couple hours later Dianne came out to run some errands. She too was use to seeing her asleep on the stairs. This time was different and she cocked her head curiously at the odd angle of her daughters head and knew. A wave of relief swept through her realizing her hard life was over. She abandoned her run and went inside to call the coroner. It took several calls over several hours before someone came to collect the corpse. Her next call was to Megan's voicemail to be the bearer of the bad news.

· · · ·

"GOOD, NO GREAT WORK guys!" Marisol said once Carmichael finished briefing the squad on their latest development. The rest of the crew had been working too and they were close to closing their first case. The entire task force was closing in on cases but the race was on to be first.

Megan pasted a phony smile on her face as she listened to her partner speak. The smile his the envy as she wished it was her up there with all eyes on them. She cast a glance at Marisol and wanted to be her as well. Except without all the milage on her vagina.

"So with any luck, we'll arrest Rico and his whole crew early like a Sunday morning," Marisol concluded. As soon as they broke up they went to handle personal business before reconvening later in the day.

"Pretty boy Floyd," Megan smiled as she checked her voicemail. He was the only one who left voice mails. Her smile vanished as she listened to her grandmother give the somber news. She let out a sigh and headed over to the Bronx. She felt bad but only because she didn't feel bad. At least she didn't have to stop by the ATM machine.

"Sup Megan. Sorry to hear about your moms," Na-Na said as Megan got out of her car in the parking. Megan nodded her thanks and rushed inside to comfort her grandmother.

"Hey grandma. You OK?" she asked in a huff from her sprint up the stairs."Yeah, just relieved I guess?" she replied and pondered again where she went wrong. She made mistakes in life but Michelle chose the road to destruction on her own. No one could save her from herself.

The women sat in virtual silence until the courtyard exploded in activity from the kids returning home in shifts. First the noisy elementary students ripping and running through the playground. They were followed by middle school kids who fought daily to establish themselves. Last the high school kids returned home.

"Hey Megan, grandma," Jax greeted as he barrelled into the apartment. He was already sweaty and winded from play on the way home but ready to go outside and formally play.

"Sup Miguel," Megan sighed and accepted his hug. He hugged his grandmother next and felt her tremor.

"What's wrong grandma?" he pulled back and asked. He had a slight protective scowl on his face ready to battle what ever was bothering his granny.

"Your mom, passed. I'm sorry," she offered softly. Both women watched closely for his reaction since he didn't really know the woman.

"When? I seen her this morning. She was sleep in the staircase," he said, pointing in that direction.

"Wow," Dianne said knowing she was dead when he saw her. "She um died right after that."

"OK. Well, I'm going downstairs." he said and turned down the hall. He stripped and switched into his play clothes and headed back out. He paused to hug the women once more in case they needed one and went to go play.

"I'm gone too," Megan announced an hour of silence later. It was time to meet her partner and go back to work.

Chapter 18

"You sure you OK?" Carmichael asked for a third time. She asked once when she picked Megan up and saw the stoic look on her face, then once more as she stared off into space during the ride uptown and now again as they sat in silence in the living room.

"Huh? Yeah, I'm good," she said and went back inside of her head. She just couldn't believe how her life turned. She could remember the nice house and nice life back on Long Island like her mom and dad taking her to the buffet and mall, her clean happy school, and a quiet backyard instead of a noisy courtyard. A knock on the door interrupted her thoughts once more.

"I got it," Carmichael offered since she didn't want her to scare whoever it was away with the look on her face.

"Sup, yo. Just came to check you out," a dude named Poncho explained his uninvited presence. He did wink at her when she came through and she winked back. That was all the invitation he needed. He held up a brown bag of malt liquor as a passport to some pussy.

"Come on in!" she cheered seeing a blunt behind his ear. She stepped aside and let him enter.

"Sup," he nodded to Megan's exposed legs then looked up to her face. He heard she was the dike so he wasn't surprised when she snarled instead of speaking. Megan was the talk of the projects for not fucking just as Carmichael was for fucking.

"Fire it up," Carmichael demanded and went to get glasses for the beer. Her black, ass cleavage jiggled from the bottom of her booty shorts as she walked. Poncho watched then watched Megan watch too and confirmed she was a lesbian.

Megan was on autopilot as they drank, smoke and laughed along to the inane chatter. Her mind was a million miles away as Poncho revealed more than he should about the operations. Good thing Carmichael's phone was recording the conversation because she didn't hear a word of it. A large shipment would be smuggled to Rico's house before the party. His distributors would all be in the house ready to leave with their fare share.

"Let me eat your pussy?" Poncho whispered loud enough to be heard across to the love seat where Megan sat alone. Carmichael replied by standing and leading him into her bedroom.

"I'm out," Megan announced to herself and left the apartment. She pretended like she was just going for a random ride but aimed the Jetta towards Manhattan. Her phone just happened to dial a familiar number.

"Megan?" Floyd asked sitting straight up in bed. He looked at the hour and asked, "You OK?"

"Um, yeah. You busy? I was gonna swing by," she said and pressed the gas pedal a little harder. "I'm crossing 159th now."

"Um," he said looking down at his company sound asleep. "Nah, I'm not busy come on."

"Huh? What's wrong?" the pretty, rookie asked as Floyd shook her awake. She spread her legs assuming he wanted a little more of that good Korean poontang.

"You gotta go. I gotta run. My um, yeah. Come on!" he said thrusting her clothes at her. He pulled some sweat pants on and a shirt while she dressed in confusion. He hustled out and over to her car and gave her a peck on her lips. "I'll call you."

"OK, I... " she tried to reply but he turned and rushed back into his building.

Megan pulled into her spot just as she pulled out and drove home to lower Manhattan. Floyd just finished changing the sex drenched sheets when she rang his bell.

"Come in!" he shouted on his way to open it. She heard him and let herself in.

"What's..."

Megan ignored his greeting and walked right past him and into his bedroom. She stopped by his bed and stepped out of her little clothes and climbed on and spread her lovely legs. He took a second to appreciate her fine frame.

"Eat me. Please. I need you to make me feel good," she pleaded almost urgently. She didn't have to ask him once and certainly wouldn't have to ask him twice. He slid between her legs face first like it was home plate and flicked his tongue on her clit.

"Sss," she said.

"Mmhm," he nodded knowingly as he munched her sweet vagina. She was so backed up she came a minute later. He would have gone for seconds until she made her next request.

"Make love to me. Real slow," she said and pulled him up. He reached for a condom from the basket of assorted condoms on his nightstand but she reached down and guided him inside of her.

Floyd felt a sense of pride when she grimaced from the pain of him entering her. She was just as tight as she had been last time they were together months earlier. She wouldn't admit it even to herself but this was his pussy. As such he treated it special and stroked it nice and easy.

"Mmm," she moaned as ecstasy replaced the pain. She wrapped her legs around his back causing him to bottom out in her box. His was a side-to-side, wiggle and drag, stroke that made her feel good as requested. She let out a guttural howl when an orgasm crept up on her.

Floyd stifled his own pleasure, which only made it worse. Megan realized he was at the point of no return and shoved him out just as he began to release.

"Don't cum in me! Are you damn crazy? I swear you better not have got me pregnant again!" she fussed as he bust on her stomach.

"Huh?" he asked, trying to reconcile her words.

"Nothing! Just get off me!" she fussed and rolled out of his bed. She pulled her clothes on despite being drenched in semen and stormed towards the door. She ignored his pleas and left his apartment.

"What you mean, again?" he asked as she marched down the hallway. She flipped him off and ducked into the stairs.

"You stupid," Megan laughed at herself as she drove back up to Sound View. She shook her head at poor Floyd. The look on his face when she mentioned pregnant took her by surprise. It was almost like he liked it. The thought was over taken by the fact that it was a fifty-fifty chance Gerald got her pregnant.

Megan turned the music up and loud as it would go to drown out her thoughts. It worked and her mind was clear by the time she reached the projects. She ignored the cat calls from the graveyard shift dope boys and entered her building.

"Still?" she asked shaking her head at the sounds of sex emanating from Carmichael's room. She posted up on the sofa to watch some TV since she was too wired for sleep. She cocked her head curiously at the half a blunt in the ashtray. She couldn't come up with a reason not to light it so she did. A few minutes later she was as smiles and giggles as she watched reruns.

The sexual symphony reached a crescendo and exploded in mutual moans of pleasure. Minutes later the door opened and the couple stepped out. Megan did a double take at Poncho who wasn't Poncho anymore. She cocked her head at Carmichael for explanation.

"Oh hey, Na-Na. This is Wink. I thought you was gone for the night with your girlfriend?" she explained. The only explanation was she was a full-fledged thot.

"I see," Megan laughed and extended the blunt to her. She took it at walked him to the door. They tongue kissed once more before she let him out and locked the door behind him. The girls smoked in silence then adjourned to their rooms. They had briefing in the morning before taking care of personal business and meeting up later for another day of surveillance.

• • • •

"OK, PEOPLE. SATURDAY night is party time!" Marisol cheered at the double entendre. It was the night of the party but they were set to make their first arrest of the task force.

The plan was to pick off the individual distributors as they left the party loaded with dope. Then they would raid the main house in the wee hours of the night. That meant Megan needed to spend the night at the house. She planned to do just that but still had no intention on having sex with him. Like grandma said, the promise of pussy is worth more than the pussy.

"You girls go handle your business and catch up later," Marisol told the girls.

"One more night," Megan sighed with relief. Carmichael let out a lonely sigh at leaving all the attention but was excited about making the first case in a month's time. All the other squads were still a month away from their first bust.

"Yup, catch you later," she said with a fist bump. She went up to the suburbs for a nap while Megan went for a funeral.

It really wasn't much of a funeral since she just picked up her mother's ashes from the crematory. Dianne placed them on the bookshelf and sighed.

"The culmination of one's life should not end in a jar on the shelf," she said thoughtfully. A lone tear escaped but she knocked it off her face before it could reach the bottom.

Megan strained her brain for appropriate words but none came. It burned her that that woman left her children like she did. She turned away before she got angry and cursed the dearly departed. The dope boys on the bench brought a smile to her face when she looked down at them. She had the goods on Nasty and the entire operations. Drugs, weapons, assaults and murders. She planned to present the whole case to the squad on Monday morning. The projects would be safe for children to play without witnessing gunfights and blowjobs.

Chapter 19

"**O**ne of the perks of being undercover," Carmichael cheered as she and Megan shopped for the party. The city had to foot the bill for clothes, shoes and purses they got to keep.

"Yeah cuz I would have to just wear some sweat pants if I had to pay for this stuff!" Megan grimaced at the high priced clothing. "This is two hundred dollars!"

"And worth every penny! That shit is fierce!" she said as Megan stepped out of the dressing room in a little black dress. It dipped low in front allowing a marvelous display of yellow titty meat. It hugged her like a mother's love and showed off all her curves.

"It is!" she blushed at the sex pot in the mirror. The city was just going to have to be out two hundred because she had to have it. Shoes and purse ran another couple hundred and she was set. "I ain't gone be able to wear no panties or anything in this!"

"Bra neither," she said, pointing out her bra strap in the strapless dress. Her dress was even less fabric than Megan's. The sheer number gave a perfect view of her goodies wrapped in a thong.

"Oh my," Megan said as her eyes fluttered at the thought. They made their purchases and headed uptown to the projects.

The courtyard was buzzing with weekend drug traffic when they breezed through with their bags. Everyone was trying to get their drugs or money to party the night away. None of these low level dealers would be present at the party but had their own holes in the wall clubs to kick and trick in.

"That's them," a girl pointed from the midst of a pack of real hood rats. They grew up in these projects yet some new thots came around and scooped their men. They would fuck for weed and felt the pinch of new meat.

"And they got bags from Saks!" another added as if that too were an infraction.

"Light skin is my size too," one said sizing Megan up. That meant whatever was in that bag was going on her ass tonight. "Come on!"

"Shit," Megan fussed as she seen the movement from her peripheral. She gauged the distance to their building and knew they weren't going to make it. Not unless they ran, which meant they weren't going to make it.

"What?" Carmichael asked looking around. She looked right over the approaching pack of rats proving how green she really was.

"These broads about to try us. Don't pull your weapon and don't blow our cover," she warned through clenched teeth.

"So what we supposed to do?" she asked in a near panic.

"Fight," she said and turned to address the hood rats. The dealers and dwellers saw the movement and moved closer to record it on their phones.

"A-yo, who y'all bitches think y'all are coming up in our projects and fucking our baby daddies?" the spokesman barked. Barked and got bit because Megan hit her dead in her shit.

"Oh shit!" the projects proclaimed in chorus as the girl's lips practically exploded. Blood from the busted lips flew from her face and splattered them both.

Both Megan and Carmichael tucked their bags between their legs and put their backs together. They chunked with the whole pack at one time and held their own. It could have went on all day if Rico hadn't pulled up.

"Go break that shit up," he demanded, sending his new sidekick in motion. He ran over and broke it up as ordered.

"Rico said chill!" he said bringing the fight to a screeching halt. All the girls huffed and puffed but no one was injured. Except for the first one who was going to need stitches.

"A-yo, we in this building right here. Anytime any of you bitches feel like stepping to me again," Megan dared. She wasn't in character either. She meant that from the bottom of her heart.

"Yeah!" Carmichael cosigned. They picked their bags up and headed inside.

"You got a little heart huh?" Megan asked as they rode up in the elevator to their apartment.

"I was scared to death!" she admitted and cracked them both up. That was the first fight of her life beside academy training.

"Well I'll fight back to back with you anytime!" she replied as they exited on to their floor. They entered the apartment and plopped down on the sofa and love seat.

"Let's smoke one," Carmichael suggested wickedly. "We got time to kill before the party?"

"We do. We should." Megan agreed and they did. They both got giggly high and took a nap until later that night.

• • • •

"I'D HIT THAT!" MEGAN nodded at her sexy reflection. The little dress was no match for here big breast and ass. She felt a delightful naughtiness at not wearing anything under it. Her curly hair cascaded around her face like a frame for a pretty picture. She may have been anti makeup but had to admit she looked good with her face beat.

"My turn. Damn!" Carmichael announced when she came out of the lone bathroom. For some reason whoever designed most projects said 'fuck them folk' and only included one bathroom no matter how many bedrooms a unit had.

"Fuck with it," Megan laughed, daring her to compete. Carmichael nodded as if accepting the challenge and stepped inside.

"First things first," she said and reached between her legs when she got under the steaming water. She massaged her clit until her knees buckled and she came in her hand. She took a quick douche in case someone wanted to eat her out. She noticed how these hood dudes swore they didn't eat no pussy but they would drop between her legs quicker than a magic trick.

Carmichael posted a smug look on her pretty face when she squeezed into the red designer tube dress. It fit like a second epidermis making a nice contrast from her own dark skin. Any light would reveal both how sheer the fabric was and how fat her vagina was.

"You were saying..." she dared as she stepped out of the bathroom. Megan twisted her lips dubiously then began to nod and clap.

"You ma'am are one bad bitch!" she conceded.

"That makes two of us. Now let's go put this clown out of business," she announced. She may have been a thot but was still a good cop and wanted nothing more than to close their case.

The hood rats were still posted up outside when the women exited the building. They all turned their heads and pretended not to see them after Rico spreaded the word to leave them alone. The one with the mouthful of stitches mumbled something to herself as they passed by.

As promised, Marisol had another vehicle on standby for them. They drove to a local gas station and switched from the Jetta into a BMW SUV and followed the GPS while the DEA tracked their movement.

"Nice," Megan nodded as they pulled up to a new build on a quiet street. No doubt this is where the drug dealer laid his head away from the projects. The music could be heard booming like some hood affair and a valet of parked cars. Mainly so they could be loaded with dope for distribution.

"Mmhm," Carmichael agreed but she meant the handsome, well-dressed men in attendance. There were plenty of pretty women in the place too. Pretty women are a dime a dozen so these two dimes took their place amongst the dozens of dimes.

"Ladies," a waiter greeted with a slight bow and tray of champagne. Both girls nodded and lifted a flute from the tray.

"Lady," Megan mocked him as she toasted with Carmichael. As soon as she sipped she saw Rico staring at her. He was engaged in an animated conversation with his team but locked eyes with her.

Got this nigga she thought to herself and fluttered her eyes coyly. Carmichael was in awe of her skills when she watched her bag a man without uttering a word.

"Let's go dance," Megan suggested and led the way to a make shift dance floor where guys and girls were dancing. They joined the other sets of girls dancing with each other while sipping Dom.

"Looks, like, you have, an admirer?" Carmichael said as she shimmied and shook in the tight dress. It must have looked like how a worm on a hook looks underwater to a fish because dudes were certainly biting.

"You do too," Megan said noticing all the guys watching her partner. She then noticed the girl Carmichael pointed at with a nod. The caramel colored woman looked about her age and wore a colorful mini dress similar to the one Carmichael wore. She flashed a smile and winked one of her green eyes. Megan initially frowned until she remembered she was supposed be gay. She smiled and winked back and turned her back.

"May I?" a gentleman asked as took Carmichael aside to grind on her. The woman took her chance and approached.

"Hello, I'm Darla," she said dancing with her from a distance.

"Megan," she replied and closed the distance between them since Rico was watching. Darla smiled and placed her hands on her hips. Most eyes watched as the seductive foreplay on the dance floor.

Meanwhile dealers began leaving one by one so they could get their product on the street. They all got knocked off one by one at various traffic stops along the way. Megan watched as the man Carmichael danced with escorted her upstairs. That was her ticket to stay while Megan awaited hers. She wouldn't have to wait long.

"Both of you come on," Rico said to both women and turned to leave with a bottle of champagne in one hand and a bottle of cognac in the other.

They followed him up the stairs like he knew they would. He led them down the hall to the master suite and closed the door behind them.

"Thank you," Megan said when he passed her a thick blunt and lighter. He nodded and passed Darla a mirror with neat lines of cocaine. She thanked him to and inhaled one up each nostril.

Megan lit the blunt and took a deep pull. She was hoping Darla would pass the mirror back to him but no such luck. Her mind raced for a plan but none came before Darla passed the mirror and straw to her. There was no choice so she inhaled two lines of her own. She fought the urge to look around even though she was quite sure she just felt the earth shift.

The weed, alcohol and cocaine circulated among small talk as Rico stripped down to his boxer briefs. Megan recalled seeing his dick almost a decade before in the darkened theatre.

"Come out them clothes. Let me see something," he ordered and leaned back against his headboard.

Both women slipped from their skimpy clothing and joined him back on the bed. Megan had to play it by ear but hoped he wouldn't end up inside of her. She tensed when Darla leaned forward and kissed her. She relaxed the instant her tongue slipped inside of her mouth. Megan got so wet so fast she felt her fluids run from inside of her. She didn't even resist when Darla laid her down and spread her legs.

"It's so pretty!" Darla marveled and her glistening vagina. Rico leaned forward to look and nodded in agreement. A lot of chicks he dealt with had a lot of miles between their legs but this one was virtually brand new.

Megan tried to hold Darla's forehead to prevent her from getting too much pussy when she dipped between her yellow thighs.

"Shit!" she fussed, feeling slightly embarrassed when her whole body bucked from the first flick of her tongue. Darla smiled wickedly knowing what was to come and moved in. Her tongue circled the swollen clitoris like a mini hurricane. The twisting tongue fucked her heterosexuality up like a twister does a trailer park. Her shoulders shrugged and feet kicked involuntarily as she sucked and licked. Now she stopped holding her head back and let her get it. Next she reached around and pulled her face deeper into her crotch by the back of her head.

"Fuck this!" Rico decided and came around behind Darla. He lifted her ass and slid inside her slippery vagina. This wasn't their first time freaking with a lesbian chick but would probably be their last.

"Oh, wow," Megan gushed as an orgasm began to wrack her mind, body and soul. She came so hard the earth shifted once more. She glanced at the clock and had mixed emotions about the time. There was still two hours before the raid so she hoped that was enough time for round two.

"Shit!" Rico announced and pulled out of Darla. He stroked himself and skeeted on her back. "Smoke break?"

"Yes!" Megan heard herself agree. She wanted another drink and a line of cocaine as well.

The trio smoked and drank in between rounds of sex. Rico had plans for his dick and didn't indulge in the coke. It had the opposite effect of cognac and stuck to that. Round two began with Darla going down on Rico. Megan watched in utter amazement at the up close and personal porn.

"Mm, let her get some," he ordered once he was rock hard once more.

"Un, uh!" Megan protested with a head shake and grimace. Rico didn't have time to work with her now and pushed back inside of her mouth. He laid on his back while she blew him and motioned for Megan to come.

"Sit on my face," he ordered and she quickly complied. He couldn't eat the pussy nowhere near as good as her but she still enjoyed it. She watched the clock and concentrated so she could get off before all hell broke loose.

It was good timing too because as soon as she came the front and back doors came flying off the hinges. As expected, everyone was drunk, sleep or fucking and cops managed to spread out quickly without any resistance.

"What the fuck!" Rico jumped up and shouted when the shouts of 'Police!' and 'Search warrant!' reached him.

Darla covered up in a sheet while Megan scrambled to get her dress on. Carmichael got caught face down with a dick in her but Megan was dressed by the time police rushed in. The subsequent search of the house turned up several drugs in large quantities as well as cash and the ever important ledgers. It had names and numbers including the one they were after: Junior Rodriquez.

Chapter 20

"Great job!" Agent Hernandez said clapping for Marisol's team as he briefed the entire task force. "All told we confiscated a million dollars in cash, and took a ton of drugs and guns!"

Megan barely heard a word that was said. She was too preoccupied with reminiscing about Darla's tongue twirling around her clit. Pretty much the same way her finger twisted around one of her curls. She shifted in her seat as she felt her panties get squishy wet from thinking about her. Luckily she got her phone number before they bonded out. Megan along with everyone else was arrested in the raid to maintain her undercover cover. They had to pull a penis out of Carmichael to put cuffs on her and her new friend.

The room erupted in applause and cheers even if most didn't mean it. In fact most were salty about being beaten by the department thot Marisol. It was well known that Marisol fucked and sucked her way up the ladder but this time she simply out copped the cops.

"So, whose next?" Major James asked from his podium. He turned his head from side to side waiting for someone to raise a hand. Megan leaned back smugly when Marisol rose her hand and stood.

"Detective Robinson has hand delivered an entire case. The projects she lives in has a booming drug trafficking operation. Murders, assaults, extortion..." The rest of the cops shot glances over at Megan as Marisol laid out the case against Nasty and the rest of the dealers. A complete case with dotted I's and crossed T's.

"Well let's get warrants and round these guys up!" the Major announced and adjourned the briefing. The teams separated and went back to their separate offices. He went to the courthouse to secure secret indictments against the drug crew. Megan knew them all so well she was able to provide legal names and addresses.

"Can I have a word with you?" Marisol asked and walked towards her office. She didn't wait for a reply since it wasn't like Megan would say 'no'.

"Sup, Sarge?" Megan said once they reached her office. She glanced around and made some mental changes for the space for when it was her office. This bust was sure to get them both promoted.

"I just wanted to congratulate you personally. I don't know what you did to get next to Rico but you did it. You made your case and that's all that matters. I know people say I slept my way up the ladder," Marisol said with a shrug.

"They do? I never heard... I mean, I," Megan stammered and stuttered until Marisol cut in and cut her off.

"Yeah right!" she laughed. "Shit, I don't care! It's true too. These silly tricks wanna promote me and pay me more money, come on with it! I haven't fucked for free since I was 15! Shit, who I look like? Carmichael?"

"You know about her?" Megan asked in a conspiratorial tone. She respected the blue line and wouldn't snitch on her partner.

"That's why I recruited her. I knew if I could harness her hoe, she could be useful," she admitted.

"Harness her hoe?" Megan asked cracking up. They shared a good laugh before getting back to the matter at hand.

"Real talk, chica. Do whatever you gotta do to make your case. No shame, no regrets. I'ma be chief of police out this bitch. Watch me!" she said lifting her chin confidently.

Megan nodded along with and had no doubt she wouldn't.

• • • •

"WHAT ARE YOU UP TO?" Dianne dared and squinted at her granddaughter, trying to see through her bullshit. And that's exactly what this sudden overnight trip to Six Flags was, bullshit.

"Huh? I can't treat my loved ones to a weekend getaway?" she replied and reeled real phony. She stared straight ahead as she drove because her grandmother did indeed have x-ray vision for her bullshit.

"You sure can!" Jax assured her from the back seat. He said his peace and went back to his hand held video game.

"Mmhm," Dianne hummed, twisted her lips and crossed her arms over her chest. Megan recognized it as she was done with it. Plus she knew the old lady loved roller coasters.

They pulled into their hotel just after dusk and checked in. Megan told on herself by constantly checking her watch, phone and then watch again. She barely touched her dinner even though she quite hungry.

"What, you got a date or something?" Dianne finally asked as she watched Megan play with her fries.

"Um, yeah. I gotta go back to the city, but I'll be back before we go to the park! Definitely! But if I'm not, just start without me and I'll catch up," she said making no sense.

"Mmhm," Dianne reiterated. Megan dropped her family off at the hotel and pulled out. She sped all the way back to city to prepare for the early morning raid. The projects were bustling with activity like any other Friday night. Except this was not any other Friday night. It would be the last Friday night some would see free for a long time. It could be the last Friday night ever for some.

"Sup, Megan!" Na-Na cheered a little more animated than usual because she was higher than usual.

"Sup with you?" Megan frowned. She almost asked why she was so jittery but remembered she didn't care.

"Nothing. I ain't doing nothing," she replied looking and sounding guilty.

"Yeah, a'ight," she replied and turned to leave. They had the goods on the drug crew but she still planned to do some surveillance from her window. This was her raid so she couldn't afford any surprises.

"Hole up! Yo, can I hole twenty bucks? I need to get some milk for my baby," she pleaded shifting from foot to foot in a panhandlers dance.

"Uh," Megan said trying to recall her having a newborn. Her oldest was already in the first grade. She shrugged again because again, she didn't care and parted with a twenty.

"Preciate it," Na-Na said over her shoulder and rushed straight over to the dope boys. Megan just shook her head as another one bit the dust.

"Yo, Megan!" another voice called before she could reach her building. Megan turned and saw a woman she knew rushing towards her. She paused and waited for her to catch up.

"Sup, La-La?" she asked although she had a clue what she wanted from the look in her eyes. That far away, shifty gaze of a junkie. Both coming and going at the same time.

"Let me hole a twenty," she said doing the beggars boogaloo. Megan was already going back into her pocket to retrieve the money. She generally wouldn't give known addicts a coin, but today was a special occasion. Today she put the drug trade in these projects out of business forever.

"Here you go," she said pressing the present into her palm. "You just missed your daughter."

La-La took off and copped some rocks and joined Na-Na upstairs to smoke crack. Megan went up to her apartment and kept watch over her impending case. She was relieved to see everything ran just as it always had. The dealers slung crack, weed and pills from their bench. They ran in and out of Nasty's building to swap out cash for drugs.

No one seemed to notice the undercover cops dressed as addicts who came to buy drugs. Megan spotted them easily by the color of the day. Each wore a yellow something to identify them to each other. Meanwhile their marked money had been circulating for days.

"Team one, 10-12," team one chimed in on the radio. They were quickly followed by the other teams as they took position in and around the projects. Half the local precinct was out in force to back up the task force.

Megan suited up in all black, bulletproof vest and ski mask, rushed out to join her team.

"Team 5, 10-12," she announced as she met up with her fellow officers. She had the honor of joining the team assigned to take Nasty into custody.

"Go! Go!" the commander commanded and the raid commenced.

"Five-O!" the screams echoed as the housing projects flooded with police. Dealers tossed guns and drugs and tried to flee but there was nowhere to run to. Everywhere they ran there was a cop ready to cuff them up.

"Shit!" Nasty shouted when he saw the commotion down below. He was caught down bad in the stash house full of drugs and money. He scrambled to shove as much cash into a bag as he could. He grabbed a pistol and hit the door trying to get down the hall to the apartment where he laid his head.

"Freeze!" Megan shouted when Nasty burst out of the apartment. "Gun!"

"Chill, I... " Nasty attempted to say as he attempted to raise his hands in surrender. Unfortunately one of his hands contained a gun and the cops gunned his ass down.

Megan aimed and sent three shots that bursted down the hall. They slammed into his chest along with twelve other rounds from the other cops. The cops cuffed the corpse and rushed inside to clear the apartment. An hour later, thirty dealers were in custody. Two more were dead and a bunch of money and drugs confiscated. A bunch of junkies got caught in the net but most would be let out with tickets to come back to court.

"May as well start calling you Sarge now," Marisol whispered as the success of the raid came to light.

"Sure thing, Lieutenant," Megan whispered back with a conspiring smile. They were both right because both had promotions in their future.

"Good job, chica. Go get some rest," she said officially and gave an unofficial fist bump.

"Rest? I gotta go to Six Flags," she sighed and shook her head. They bumped fist and went their separate ways.

Megan rushed back down the Jersey Turnpike and eased back into the hotel room. Dianne opened one eye to peek at her granddaughter sneaking around the room. She could smell the gunpowder on her as she slipped into the bathroom to shower. Megan eased into the bed next to her and went to sleep.

Jax popped up bright and early, ready to go. Megan was dog tired but rolled out of bed and got dressed. They spent the next twelve hours riding roller coasters and eating junk food before the long ride home.

"Gonna be some changes around the projects," Megan nodded smugly as they crossed over from Manhattan to the Bronx. Dianne frowned a curious frown wondering what she could possibly mean. She'd lived in those same projects for over forty years and nothing ever changes.

"OK," she said and shrugged. She perked up in her seat as they neared the projects. Little Jax was slobbering and snoring when they pulled up.

"What the fu..." Megan whined when they pulled up in the projects. The drug trade was booming as if a raid hadn't taken place just 12 hours earlier. The only thing that changed was the faces. "Awe man!"

"I know, baby. I know," her grandmother comforted.

Chapter 21

The next year sailed by pretty smoothly. *OK, so I hooked up with Darla once or twice. OK three times before I caught myself. And yeah, I had to go see Floyd a couple times to get her off my mind. If I didn't know any better I would say he loved me. I swear he'll drop anything and anyone when I need him. And I needed him to turn me back straight again cuz Darla was about to turn my ass out.*

The squad made a ton of arrests but didn't make a dent in the drug trade. It seemed like junior junkies and dealers were on deck like a baseball game. As soon as one fell another one stepped up to take their place. 90% of the dealers we arrested gave up their supplier. The name Junior Rodriguez was at the tip of every tongue. Now the bullseye was on his back.

Oh and I made sergeant! Marisol went on an assignment and I got the squad. Me, Sergeant Robinson. Just like my dad! Then I ended up dead, just like my dad.

"OK, ladies and gentlemen. This is our target, Junior Rodriguez," Agent Hernandez announced as Junior's handsome face splashed on the large screen. "He's feeling the heat and moved his base down to Atlanta, Georgia. He obviously doesn't know we are a federal task force and we're coming with him! He's smart and it's not going to be easy to build a case."

Megan snarled dangerously knowing this was the last person her friend/mentor and big sister was seen with before she was never seen again. He was now in his early forties but could pass for a twenty something. He was handsome rich and dangerous. Smart, rich and evil.

"An undercover officer has infiltrated his organization," Hernandez said and clicked to the next picture. A collective gasp was heard when they saw Marisol snuggled up next to him by a lavish pool. She looked stunning with a bronze tan, gold jewelry and round ass hanging out of her bikini. The picture explained where she disappeared to six months back. He clicked a few more pictures taken by cops with telephoto lenses. Junior was living it up with his friends and associates.

"Wait! Go back!" Megan suddenly stood and shouted. Agent Hernandez backed the slide show up and Megan saw a familiar face.

"See someone you know?" he asked looking back and forth between her and the screen. Megan blinked rapidly at Jax lounging on a chair with a drink.

He was the only one who didn't have a scantily clad woman on his lap nor smile on his face. Instead he wore a determined scowl and greedy glare in his eyes.

"No, I thought it was... no, un uh," she said shaking her head. She felt her blood began to boil when Jax appeared in several pictures. He was always in the background and never with a woman. Megan did the math and realized her twenty fifth birthday also marked his 15th year in prison. Jax was back.

"OK, so get packed. We're going to Atlanta!" Hernandez said and wrapped up the briefing.

. . . .

"SO WHY CAN'T I GO WITH you?" Jax needed to know when Megan broke the news to him.

"Cuz, it's work," she said and braced herself for his whining. He was now a handsome, six foot two inch 15 year old with a deep voice but still whined around his big sister. "A month, two and I'll be back."

"A'ight but if I get into trouble it's your fault," he warned with a giggle.

"Only trouble I'm worried about you is and them fast ass little girls! You using condoms boy?" she fussed. She hated how handsome he'd become since he looked just like his father. She could see his face every time she closed her eyes.

"I'm not even having sex with... " he started to say until his sisters twisted lips cut it short. "Of course I'm using condoms. I'm going to the NBA and don't need nothing holding me back!"

"My nigga," she cheered and offered a fist bump. He might not make it all the way to the NBA but colleges were clamoring for him already. At the very least he had a free college education in his future. "Yo, first priority..."

"I know. Take care of grandma," he sighed. The woman still thought she was taking care of them but signs of Dementia were creeping into her world.

"A'ight, Tariq. Hold it down," she said and turned to leave. She didn't make it from the room they still shared before he hugged her. He held her tightly as if it was his last time. An awkward silence followed when he released her. She certainly couldn't tell him she was heading to Atlanta to kill his father so she ducked her eyes and rushed from the room. Dianne was sleeping so she eased a kissed on her forehead and left for the airport. The old lady opened one eye and watched her leave.

Megan's cover was a student from California. Even at 25 she could appear 18 but was posing as a 21 year old grad student named Kenneka Martin. She watched movies from Cali to pick up slang, dialect and inflection. She knew all the streets, restaurants and clubs. This was an extremely dangerous crew and nothing could be taken for granted.

"Here we go," she told herself as she pulled into the upscale, gated condo complex. The red Lexus she drove looked the part of daughter of a wealthy California lawyer.

This was the same complex Jax lived in since he moved down with the crew. Junior gave him the condo and new Bentley the moment he stepped off the plane. He was quickly promoted to number two in the operations due to his loyalty. The rest of the crew was jealous but Jax wasn't impressed. After all, no one wants to be number two.

Megan drove by her own unit and cruised through the complex to see if she could get a glimpse of her target. She volunteered to keep an eye on him but left out the part of that eye being behind the sights of her gun. She had no intentions on arresting him. She planned to put a bullet in his brain just like he did her father. After glaring at his empty parking spot she came back around the complex and parked in her own.

"Need some help?" a woman called out as Megan struggled to unpack her packed trunk. The unit was furnished and stocked but Megan was treated to a new wardrobe to match her role as well off grad student. A classy, somewhat sexy collection courtesy of the government.

"Huh?" Megan asked and cocked her head in confusion. She understood her words just fine but it was her Muslim garb that she didn't get. The woman had on a flowing overgarment and a veil covering her face except her eyes.

"I speak a couple more languages and American sign..." she replied and flashed a smile under her veil. "Portuguese? Dutch maybe?"

"I'm sorry. We don't see many Muslims in Brentwood, California! Not New York," she quickly clarified and focused on her accent.

"Um, OK, but can I help?" the woman asked reaching for her bags. Megan just shrugged since the woman was already helping. "Fatimah."

"Kenneka," Megan replied and led the way to her new unit.

"Oh, we're neighbors! I'm right upstairs," Fatimah cheered when Megan went to her unit. "I go to med school at Tech."

"Me too! Well, law school but Tech," Megan replied. She fought the urge to shout 'Damn!' when she opened the door to the condo. It was decked out with leather and chrome with all the latest electronics.

"Well, I'm upstairs if you need anything," Fatimah offered once they finished unloading the fully loaded car.

"OK, maybe we can hit a club or...well, probably not, huh?" Megan said realizing the woman probably didn't go clubbing.

"No, but I love to eat. Dinner on me tonight!" she insisted and turned to leave. Megan watched her curiously until she disappeared into her condo.

• • • •

ONCE MEGAN UNPACKED and got somewhat organized her stomach rumbled to remind her that her body had rights over her. She hopped in the glass-enclosed shower and rinsed the day away. She dried and slipped into a tasteful, knee length summer dress and sandals.

"Guess I'll take you up on your offer," she decided and hopped up the stairs. She could hear Arabic being recited as she rang the bell. The recitation stopped and the door opened. Megan squinted at the pretty, brown woman and asked "Is Fatimah here? I'm the girl who moved in downstairs. We was going to get dinner?"

"It's me. Come on in," she said with a chuckle. Most people didn't recognize her since she was rarely seen without her veil when out and about.

"Oh, OK. Um," she said and entered the condo. Megan noticed she looked around her age and had quite the figure in the shorts and tank top she wore around her house. Her natural hair was pulled into a curly ponytail giving her a clean, well groomed look. She nodded at the nice furnishings in the unit as Fatimah stepped in her room to get dressed. A few moments later she emerged in full garb once more.

"Ready?" she asked and picked up her plain purse and keys. Megan nodded and followed her out to a brand new Cadillac CTX. She pressed the key fob and the car hollered back by a honk and flash of its lights

"So, where you from?" Megan asked, expecting her to say Mauritania, Dubai or somewhere exotic.

"Newark. New Jersey," she added just in case she wasn't sure which one. "I went to Rutgers for undergrad."

"Oh, OK," Megan said. She didn't realize it was her turn to state where she went for undergrad studies. "So, you like Atlanta? It's my first time."

"It's nice. Especially coming from the hood. My parents own a few houses up there. They sold one and got the condo for me. I'm trying to get them to move down to but they stubborn."

"I can relate," Megan sighed. Her own mother was pretty stubborn. She wouldn't leave the dope alone until it killed her. They traded questions along the way in an effort to get to know each other. Each answer revealed how much they had in common as they inched towards friendship. Besides Floyd, she would be her first friend.

"So, why you gotta dress like that?" Megan asked once her and Fatimah got seated in the upscale seafood restaurant. Once they were seated Fatimah flipped the veil up and revealed her pretty face. "Your parents make you dress like that?"

"Nah, God," she said and paused to chew her salad. She could tell from the look on her face she expected her to expound. She finished chewing, swallowed and did just that. "Islam requires modesty from both male and females. God orders us to cover our beauty except for husband and family. So modesty is mandatory but the veil isn't. I chose to wear it to keep dudes out my face."

"Makes sense," Megan said tilting her head from side to side to help process the new information. She didn't cover to that degree but didn't dress like a prostitute like popular fashion dictated either. "So, why y'all can't eat pork? I don't either but I'm just asking."

"Cuz God said don't eat it," she replied with a shrug. "Many Muslims will answer that question with stuff about pigs being part rat or trichinosis but the truth is much simpler than that. God said don't eat it and that's that."

"Just cuz God said so..." Megan repeated and nodded. "I like that! Just cuz God said so and that should be enough."

Chapter 22

"Jax! My man!" Junior cheered when Jax entered the den of his plush home in an upscale Atlanta suburb. He was indebted to the man who got his father out of his way so he could take the reigns. Marisol lifted off of him and walked away so they could talk before he got the chance to dismiss her. The man was too smart to talk on the phone or in front of people. As guarded as he was publicly he was quite the chatter box in private. Their pillow talk after sex contained enough info to put him away for several lifetimes.

"What's good," Jax replied and watched her ass jiggle in the tiny Japanese style robe. She may have been laced in all the latest fashions but she didn't wear much clothing around the house. Junior was addicted to putting his dick in her and clothes just slowed down the process.

"Bruh, you like that, huh? Well get your own!" Junior ordered as he watched him watch her ass. "You still ain't got no ass since you came home?"

"Nah. Shit I got so much pussy in prison, thanks to you, I'm not really pressed. I'm holding out for my queen," he said. He did keep him stocked with all the comforts of home while he was away. Including a steady supply of nurses, counselors and female guards to service him orally and vaginally. Junior nodded understandingly, not understanding he intended to be the king. Jax was watching and waiting for his chance to take the crown. If his head came off in the process, so be it.

Marisol certainly was fine but he didn't want his hand me downs. He planned to empty the entire house and redecorate once he took the reigns. That included his own fine young chick to keep by his side. Junior served his purpose and built the empire. He was also reckless enough to get himself hot as fire. Jax would put him in a box and take over from here.

"Well, maybe you'll find her tonight," he said since they partied every night. Jax only hung out so he could get info the operations. So far Junior kept him at arms length from the action. He chunked piles of cash at him but kept him hands off. Until now that is as he contemplated his retirement.

"I doubt it but we'll see what happens," he said and reached for the blunt Junior extended towards him. He took a shallow toke but didn't inhale. Meanwhile, Marisol took the opportunity to make a quick call.

• • • •

"HELLO?" MEGAN ASKED as she answered the unknown number her phone.

"Hey, Kenneka. This is Safiya," Marisol said and paused to make sure they were on the same page.

"Oh, hey girl. What's good?" she said as she caught the voice. Marisol was deep undercover and now could introduce Megan into the crew. She realized they needed another way in since Junior didn't show her much besides his dick.

"Nothing much, chica. My man is having a party at the Ritz tonight. I'll make sure you're on the guest list," she informed. She would have to catch her face to face to brief her since Junior kept cameras and microphones all over the house. Mainly to record their frequent sex but a few scheming employees got caught lying or stealing. Most got fired by firing squad and never seen again.

"I'll be there!" she cheered and hung up. She turned her attention back to the chess board as if never interrupted.

"Be where?" Fatimah asked and put her in check. The two hung out daily and grew closer by the day. Megan taught her to play chess and now she was beating her. She taught Megan subtle life lessons in return. Megan loved watching and listening to her when she offered her daily prayers. She didn't understand the words but felt the peace and tranquility that descends anytime God is remembered and glorified.

"A party. A friend of mines boyfriend is throwing one. You wanna come?" Megan quipped with a sarcastic smirk. She knew full well her friend wasn't going anywhere near a nightclub.

"Will they let me wear my veil or will I need some booty shorts?" she shot back with a straight face. "I wonder can I twerk in my overgarment?"

"Probably not," she said shaking her head. She genuinely would rather stay there and hang out with her new friend but had a job to do. "Check."

"Make that checkmate," Fatimah corrected and trapped her King. Megan acquiesced with a slight curtsy and stood.

"I'll see you tomorrow, home girl," she said and extended her fist for bumping.

"Later tator," she said with a bump. Fatimah got up as well to lock the door behind her as she went downstairs to get dressed.

• • • •

"SHOLE WISH FLOYD WAS here," Megan admitted when she washed between her legs in the shower and a shiver shot up her spine. She knew she needed some relief and sat the washcloth down. A few minutes later she massaged herself to a squealing orgasm. "Whew!"

With that out the way her mind was clear so she turned her attention on what to wear. She hadn't had any luck spotting Jax yet but was pretty sure he would be at the party. She planned to wear something sexy in hopes of luring him somewhere so she could kill him.

It was a good plan except none of her sexy clothes had room for a pistol. The dress she chose couldn't contain all of her titties so it definitely couldn't hold a gun. She still took an unregistered 40 caliber with her and tucked it under her seat. Megan followed the directions to the club and let the valet take her car away.

"Kenneka Martin," she informed the bouncer who checked her breast, then his list. He nodded as both met his approval and he lifted the velvet rope so she could enter. He locked in on her round ass jiggling under the dress as she went inside. The thong was the next best thing to naked and her ass jumped and wiggled when she walked

"Wow!" Megan exclaimed as she entered the packed club. Several dance floors were jammed with gyrating bodies. Many were dry humping and tongue kissing. A prelude to a one night stand or next baby daddy. Megan didn't have a clue which way to go but luckily Marisol spotted her and made her way through the sea of people.

"Hey, girl!" she said giving her a hug and escorting into the bowels of the establishment.

"Hey, Safiya. You look great!" Megan gushed as they kissed cheeks and hugged. Her left tittie bounced out of her dress but she tucked it back in quickly before anyone could see it. Not that anyone would care with all the exposed tits and ass.

Marisol immediately steered her straight one of the many bathrooms for a quick briefing. The bathrooms had as much going on inside as there was outside in the club. A couple of fems tongue kissed up against a wall. One dropped her head to an exposed titty and slipped a hand under her short dress. "Oh my!"

"Yeah, they get their freak on in here," Marisol said looking for a place to speak. They tried a stall but found it occupied by a woman eating another woman's pussy. The scene made Megan pause and think of Darla, which made her vagina thump. The next one was empty so they ducked inside.

"Listen, Junior is planning to turn the operations over to his friend, Jax. I'm not getting anything out of him but cum and money. Jax is looking for a wife. You're up!"

"Nothing?" Megan asked cocking her head in confusion. The team was certain he was the brains of the operations. They had almost a hundred witnesses ready to testify against him. All they had to do was catch him with something, anything and his ass was going under the jail.

"Nah, I been with him six months and haven't seen drugs, guns, money, nothing!" she vowed minus the eye contact. "What I do know is Jax was running the show from prison. They all just using Junior as the fall guy because of who his father was,"

"Wow," Megan squinted as she tried to picture this bullshit Marisol was feeding her. She remembered O'Neil's dairy and knew he was the last one to see her alive. Still, she has her chance to get next to Jax and that's all that mattered. "Well, OK. Let's get it then."

"Let's!" Marisol cheered and led the way out of the bathroom. Megan snuck a glance at her ass as it shook in front of her, not knowing hers was just as spectacular.

"Here comes my baby!" Junior said and stood when they reached his table. Megan saw the look in his eye and now understood. They were obviously in love. He was utterly pussy whipped and she, dick and dough whipped.

"This is my friend, Kenneka. I know her from home but it's hard to get miss goodie two shoes out the house," she said by way of introduction. Jax leaned up when he heard 'goody two shoes'. He had no interest in the thots that threw themselves at him everyday.

Megan froze when they locked eyes. She had a vision of breaking one of the champagne flutes and stabbing him in his neck. They both stood there staring at each other for a minor eternity.

"Looks like you found your queen, papa!" Junior cheered and cheesed at the obvious love connection.

"I'm Jax," he said standing and peering down at her. He squinted at the familiarity but it didn't register. She looked enough like her father for him not to remember fucking her mother.

"Kenneka," she said and flinched when he extended his hand. She felt a cold chill run up her spine when he leaned down to kiss her hand. She couldn't help but wonder if this was the hand that killed her father. Or was it the other. It really didn't matter as he was shaking the hand that would end his life.

"You OK, girl?" Marisol warned, since she was acting strange. Megan shook her head to clear the murderous thoughts and smiled.

"I am now," she replied looking up into Jax's eyes. He was fifteen years her senior but prison had him looking like a thirty year old. The two sat and began to converse as she slipped back into character.

"Champagne?" Jax asked reaching for a bottle from the ice bucket.

"I don't drink," Megan offered almost apologetically, not knowing she just scored more points with her target. Jax didn't want any woman who drank, smoked or fucked on the first date. The two sat and chatted over the chatter of the club for hours. Neither budged when Junior and Marisol stood to leave. It was another hour before Megan left his intense gaze.

"I have to use the bathroom," Megan whined when her bladder couldn't wait any further. "You mind?"

"I'm not going anywhere," Jax assured her as he peered into her eyes. As long as she didn't fuck him tonight he was sure he found his queen. She looked demur and out of place even in the sexy dress. He locked eyes on her ass as she departed. A slight wobble in the high heels proved she wasn't use to wearing them as well. Most club chicks could run, jump and screw in a six-inch heel.

"Bout to pee on myself!" Megan groaned as she squeezed through the packed club. It seemed like people jumped in her way to block her path. Like they wanted her to pee on herself. She began pushing and shoving as the situation grew dire. "Excuse, me!"

"Excuse you is right!" a woman reeled in response to being pushed in her back. She reeled around ready to fight then squinted. "Megan?"

"Nah," Megan shot quickly and winced from the alcohol on her breath. It was her turn to squint when she recognized her cousin, Angel. "Wrong person!"

"Wrong person?" she frowned. She was drunk but certain this was her family and fell in step after her, calling her name. "Megan, it's me! Angel, your cousin. Megan!"

"Bitch gonna blow my damn cover," she fumed as she went as quickly as she could through the human quick sand. A glance over her shoulder showed Jax was watching her and Angel was closing in. She barely made it into the bathroom when she caught her.

"Megan, that is you?" she slurred and pointed inches from her face. "It's me, Angel. Your cousin."

"Shit! Come in here," she said and pulled her into a stall. "Yeah, it's me but shhhh! I can't talk right now,"

"I saw you in VIP and thought it was you! Take me with you so I can meet a baller. Don't be no hater!" she insisted. "I'm tryna meet me a baller too!"

"Chill. I'll call you tomorrow and..."

"Hell no! You ain't cock blocking like you did when we went on that date! I'm coming with you to VIP. I'ma get me one of them ballers!" she shouted in a drunken rage. It was bad enough but got worse when she remembered, "Ain't you a police now? I heard...ugh!"

Megan snatched Angel by her neck to shut her up before she blew her cover. She resisted but her struggle ended when Megan put her in a classic LAPD choke hold. She then squeezed the struggling and kicking woman until she relaxed and went limp in her arms. She squeezed a little more just to be sure and gently sat her on their toilet.

"Now you... shit!" she fussed when she saw the far away gaze of the dead in her eyes. She shook her head at her dead cousin and shrugged. "Told your ass to chill."

Megan realized she peed herself and shook her head some more. She had no choice now but to leave since she couldn't go back to him wet. Jax saw her come out of the bathroom and make a beeline to the door. He watched curiously as she departed without saying a word.

"Fuck that!" he told himself and followed her out. She was just pulling away when he emerged from the club. He shoved his ticket to the valet but accepted defeat. No way he could catch her since he had no idea which way she went. He let out a frustrated sigh until he recalled she was Safiya's friend. "I do believe I found my queen."

Chapter 23

"**S**hit!" Megan fussed in reply to the urgent knock on her door the next morning. She just knew it was Atlanta PD coming to arrest her for murder. She was ready to go after staring at her dead cousin's eyes all night. She'd choked her out several times every time she'd drifted off to sleep. Jail would be a relief. Her only regret was not getting to kill Jax first. She opened her door and got the shock of her life. "What the..."

"Delivery," the delivery man said, despite the obvious. He held a large arrangement of flowers while several more delivery men brought more from the truck. The opulent display brought most of her neighbors to their doors and windows including Fatimah.

"Girl, what you got going on?" she dared, while trying to secure her scarf on her head, "Is this why you didn't get in 'til 2 am?"

"I..." she replied, completely overwhelmed. Megan had never gotten a flower before in her life, so a thousand blew her mind. She signed for the delivery and read the card. She tilted her head curiously at the name, Jax.

"And who is...Jax?" her friend demanded as she read over her shoulder.

"He's..." she began and paused. Somehow saying he was a handsome, debonair, funny guy she planned to kill just didn't seem appropriate, "a guy."

"Mmhm," Fatimah hummed daringly, "A guy that sends thousands of dollars worth of flowers wants to be more than just "a guy.""

Megan shrugged and went back inside just in time to catch her ringing phone. She frowned at the unknown number and took the call, "Hello?"

"But, no goodbye. You left without saying goodnight," Jax said, sounding just as good on the phone as he did in person.

"Who is this?" she fussed just as she should have. Jax smiled at her defensive posture to an unnamed man on her phone.

"Jax, from the club," he said and awaited her reaction.

"Oh! Hey! I'm sorry about last night. I'm really not used to guys and well..." she replied.

"And that's even more reason to get to know me. Let me take you to lunch," he offered.

"I have plans with my neighbor. How about dinner?" she asked eagerly.

"It's a date! I'll pick you up at six," he said and hung up.

"But , I didn't tell you where I live," Megan frowned. She knew it had to be Marisol, so she dialed her number.

"Hey, Kenneka," Marisol greeted. She put the phone on speaker to free her hands to continue massaging Junior's feet. "Guess who came asking about you first thing this morning."

"I'm guessing same guy who sent me a thousand flowers and just asked me out to dinner," she said. Junior didn't like sharing his woman's attention so he whipped out his dick for some attention.

"Speaking of dinner, my lunch has just been served. I'll see you later," she said and clicked off. Marisol kissed her way up his muscular legs until she had him in her mouth. He gently played in her hair while she blew him.

"I been thinking about what you said, and I'm going to do it. We'll fly down to Belize and I'll introduce Jax to the plug. Then we can retire and do this every day.

"Sounds like a plan," she paused to say. She would have said more, but he guided himself back into her mouth. This was no time for talking.

• • • •

"OH MY GOD, ISN'T THAT the club you went to last night?" Fatimah screeched and pointed at the news report of a woman found strangled in a bathroom stall.

"Huh? I'm not...sure," she said, squinting at the TV as if she couldn't see the sign plain as day. She tuned in as reports speculated about some kinky sex play gone wrong. Semen would definitely be found in Angel whenever the autopsy was done.

"See, that's why you have no business in those places!" she fussed at her friend.

"You're right. I won't be going there ever again. I'm going to dinner with the guy I met. Just dinner, no booty," she assured her with a laugh.

"Well, if you need a chaperone..." she offered seriously, "Anytime a man and a woman are alone the devil is a third party."

"Yeah," Megan nodded. She didn't need the devil to urge her to do wrong tonight. She could put a bullet in his brain all by herself.

The two friends kicked it for several more hours, until it was time for Megan to get ready for her date. She then went back downstairs and walked straight into the shower. She had no desire to look cute for the man who'd murdered her father, but it was unavoidable since she was a cute girl.

"I'm almost ready!" she called out to the knock on her door. She noticed he was early as she headed to open it. "You're early."

"No, just in time," Special Agent Hernandez said, stepping inside.

"W-w-wh-what are you doing here? The target is on his way to pick me up," Megan asked, but the look on his face said all that needed to be said. "You know don't you?"

"I know. I'm surprised you're willing to throw your career away over a need for revenge," he said as he sat down on the sofa. He put his feet up on the coffee table, letting her know he wasn't going anywhere.

"I could have killed him already, if that's what I wanted to do," she said matter of factly. "We're close to shutting the whole operation down!"

"Bullshit! Ruiz has been completely compromised and you're on a revenge mission. It's over! Case closed! I can't afford to lose another good cop." Megan sank to the sofa under the heavy words. She was a good cop and almost did throw it all away. She wondered what her father would do in her shoes. She nodded along to the answer she knew all too well. He would have done his job.

"Junior Rodriquez is turning the operations over to Jax. In a matter of days I can have enough on him to send him back to prison for the rest of his life. Pull me out now and Marisol will warn Junior. We have enough witnesses already to put him under the jail. Let me do my job."

"Do it. You have a week!" he said and stood. He had done his homework on her and had no doubt she would do just that. Her phone rang again and *Dead Dog* popped up on her screen.

"Don't mind that," Megan giggled in embarrassment and took Jax's call. Hernandez shook his head as she slipped back into character. "Hello? You are? Okay, I'll be right out."

"I'll let myself out," he said as she grabbed her purse and keys. He waited until she left and planted a few cameras and microphones. They'd already lost Marisol and couldn't afford to lose her too. The clock was ticking and she had a week.

• • • •

"NICE," JAX SAID ALOUD as Megan stepped from her condo. He poked his bottom lip out and nodded at her tasteful full-length dress, glad she wasn't dressed like last night. Once she became his woman she could never dress like that again.

"Well, hello again," Megan sang as he came around and opened her car door. She hated to admit it but he looked even better in the light of day. "Hello yourself," he greeted with a half hug. He again misunderstood when she tensed from his kiss to her cheek. He thought it was modesty, but it was murder on her mind. He closed the door behind her and came back around the driver's side. "You like seafood?"

"Like, no I love seafood!" she gushed like a girl. That part wasn't an act since seafood brought the inner fat girl in her out.

"That's good to know. Hold that thought," he nodded thoughtfully. Their conversation picked up just like it did from the night before. Ironically, neither really experienced any of the worldly topics they bantered about. Hers came from the internet while his came from books and magazines in the prison library.

They ended up at a popular Cajun seafood restaurant just north of the city. Neither could decide so they decided to order several entrees and share them. The only breaks in the conversation came to chew or sip. Megan shook her head thinking she could actually like him if she didn't hate him.

"What?" Jax asked in reply to her terse head shake. He hoped not to get one in reply to his next question.

"Huh? Nothing, just thinking about last night. The news said a woman was found dead at the club last night! Strangled during sex," she relayed. She whispered the word *sex* just like a good girl would and Jax was smitten.

"Yeah, I saw that. But, come away with me this weekend. Belize?" he offered and gazed deep into her soul.

• • • •

"I CAN'T GO AWAY WITH a guy?" she whined and ducked coyly.

"I'm not just a, guy. I'm your guy. This may sound crazy but I'm going to marry you. I'm on the verge of being crowned king and I need a queen," he laid out smooth as jam on toast. Megan giggled ducked and nodded her head.

"OK, I'll come," she agreed. They shared a desert before Jax took her her home. The perfect gentleman placed a tender kiss on her cheek once they reached her door.

"Ugh!" Megan fussed and wiped his kiss off her face as soon as she got inside. She heard the door above her open and closed so she opened hers once more.

"Handsome, Bentley, but isn't he a little old for you?" Fatimah asked as she came in the condo.

"Yes, yes and yes," she sighed. They had become so close in the recent weeks she hated keeping secrets from her. She actually cringed when she called her Kenneka but had to keep her cover.

"Are you OK? You have the strangest look in your eye?" she said and came closer to investigate.

"No, but I will be," Megan replied. She recalled Fatimah never spoke of things to come in the future without adding 'God willing', so she added it herself. "God willing, everything will be just fine."

Chapter 24

"Hey, girl!" Marisol cheered and rushed to hug Megan's neck when she and Jax reached the airport. Traveling by private jet allowed them to bypass the long lines and checkpoints. Instead, the driver pulled directly to the hanger where Junior kept his jet.

"Hey, Safiya," she replied and returned the hug. The men shook hands and led the way on the jet. Jax nodded in approval at the plush private transportation. He had no doubt this was how Junior was importing his drugs.

"So, you guys hitting it off pretty good, huh?" she gushed as they huddled at a table so the men could talk. Megan felt her heart break when she noticed the signs of drug use on her friend. Marisol tried to play it off, but kept sniffling and pawing at her nose. Her nostrils were red and raw from snorting cocaine.

"Um, yeah," Megan admitted. They ate dinner every night and then talked for hours once he dropped her off with nothing more than a kiss on the cheek. He was so nice Megan actually pulled up his case file to make sure this was the same guy. It was paying off since he alluded to the same thing she heard from Marisol. Jax was on the verge of taking over the operation.

"That's good. He's nice," she said and sniffed the drain of cocaine in her nose.

"What are you doing?" Megan leaned in and whispered. She glanced over at the men making small talk while puffing big cigars and hoped they could talk.

"I don't know what I'm doing?" Marisol whined, tearing up. Her lip began to quiver as she fought back the tears. "I didn't mean to fall in love. Let Junior go. He quit. Jax is gonna run the show. I can help make a case against him. I know where they stash the drugs. I know where the money is..."

"I'm listening," Megan replied and leaned in to listen. Listen she did as Marisol laid out things his closest advisors didn't know about.

"She's gorgeous," Junior nodded as he looked to the front of the plane to where the woman conspired like teens. They looked back and giggled from time to time while planning Jax's demise.

"She is," Jax said and fought his jealousy. He'd claimed Megan as his own and hated him even looking at her. "I'm gonna marry her."

"That's what's up! Me and Safiya are getting married tomorrow. She just doesn't know it yet. Lots of surprises this weekend," he said and lifted his glass.

"Lots," Jax agreed as they clinked glasses. Each toasted to their own agenda and nodded.

• • • •

"SEE YOU GUYS IN THE morning," Junior announced when they reached the private villas they would be spending the weekend. He and Marisol rushed inside their suite and got straight to it. He was inside the hot Latina before Jax and Megan got inside their room.

"This is us," Jax said, pointing at the plush bungalow. Megan swallowed hard and followed him inside.

"This is beautiful!" she gushed as she took in the lavish room. It was almost pure white with a large circular bed surrounded by sheer mosquito netting. A sinking feeling contradicted her elation when she saw it was the only bed in the room.

"You're beautiful," he said and wrapped her in his arms. Once again her whole body tensed when he leaned down to kiss her. "What's wrong? You sure you want to be here? With me? I can have the jet take you home?"

"No!" she shouted at her case slipping away. "I um, I'm just tired. I just had exams and..."

"Say no more," he cut in and placed his finger to her lips. He guided her over to the bed and placed her on it. He snuggled up next to her and wrapped her in his arms. Soon they were both sound asleep.

"Mmm," Megan moaned and grinded her ass against the hard dick she woke up to. The couple times she spent the night with Floyd, the morning started just like this. He would grind back then lift her leg to slide inside her from behind. Once he got her off, he would flip her on her back and fuck her face to face. This allowed her to watch his fuck faces and push him out before he came. She liked to lean up and watch him skeet on her stomach. The pill or condoms would have been safer but less fun. She did make sure he never came in her because she vowed to never have an abortion again. One young girl from the projects ended up sterile at 17 from an abortion.

"Mmm, good morning," Jax croaked with his voice thick with desire. This isn't how he envisioned their first time to be but he would take it.

"Huh!" Megan panicked when she heard his voice and rolled off the bed. She got tangled in the netting and fell on her face. She felt utterly silly, but still tried to play it off. "Morning!"

"Good morning to you, too," he said with a chuckle. "Ready for breakfast?"

"I am. Let me get a shower," she said. She grabbed her bag and went into the bathroom and locked the door. After a strong pee she got under the rain-head shower and bathed. She then selected a pair of plain cotton panties and bra to go under a tasteful sundress.

"My turn," Jax said and stepped into the bathroom. He didn't close the door completely, and Megan tried not to look. It only lasted a few seconds before she turned her head in time to see his naked body step under the shower. She was as mesmerized now as she was when she was ten and hiding in her den. Her eyes slowly traced his muscular frame down to his dick.

"No!" she told her vagina as it began to react to the visual stimuli. It throbbed and began to moisten anyway causing her to get up and step out of the room.

"Hey!" Marisol waved and approached when she saw her step out. She had a warm glow of good sex that competed with her bright smile. The woman was as happy as she'd ever been in her life.

"Hey," Megan greeted in return. "This place is cool!"

"Thanks. He owns it, so you can come anytime you want," she gushed and leaned in for details. "So..."

"Un uh," Megan grimaced and shook her head at the thought of what the other girl was implying. She planned to fake her period later or something, anything to keep him out of her.

"Girl, he just got out. He'll probably only last a few seconds," Marisol laughed. The men emerged and she leaned in closer to whisper before they all set down to breakfast. "Do whatever you gotta do to make the case."

The four bantered over croissants, pineapple marmalade and the freshest oranges in the world. It was all so friendly, no one could tell just how badly Megan wanted to murder the man. She wasn't the only one with homicide on her mind.

"Why don't you girls go shopping? Jax and I have some business to tend to," Junior advised, when they finished their meal. He passed Marisol a roll of cash several inches thick and stood.

"Yeah, buy yourself something pretty," Jax seconded and gave Megan a similar wad of cash. Megan stared at the dirty money for a second until Marisol cleared her throat. O'Neil's words replayed in her head as she accepted the cash, *Everyone takes money.*

• • • •

"WHAT'S THIS PLACE?" Jax asked as Junior pulled to a gated estate. It had plug written all over it, but he needed to her their words that made his existence obsolete. This is what he was waiting on, hoping and plotting on.

"The plug," he replied and pulled up to the security gate. His smile granted him access and lifted the gate. Jax saw the life he wanted when they reached the circular drive filled with exotic cars. This is what he just spent 15 years of his life for. This is what he killed for and would kill again for.

Junior took him through the house and out to the pool where Rude Boy lounged by the pool. Naked women of all races were seen frolicking in the pool. Meanwhile the shirtless dred played an animated game of soccer on the video game system.

"My man Junior!" Rude boy stood and greeted. His eyes narrowed at Jax as they shook.

"Who this?"

"My right hand man, Jax. He's the one I told you about. I wanted you to meet face to face," he said as the men shook hands. They got down to the business of importing and trafficking cocaine. Junior planned to reveal his surprise to Jax once they returned to the states. Meanwhile Megan and Marisol got their shopping on.

"Tell me you couldn't get use to this?" Marisol dared as she did a twirl in a designer dress. The thin fabric cost a month's salary from the force.

"I could," Megan heard herself say. The beautiful scenery was intoxicating compared to the stark projects she came from. She never knew how much she liked nice things until she got to try them on. "These sandals are everything!"

"And cost more than that car you drive! We did good, chica. We deserve to live like this!" she recruited. She was content with running away with Junior, but wanted happiness for her friend, too.

"I do, but I can't. I'll turn my head to what you got going on, but Jax gotta go," Megan insisted. Marisol shrugged since she tried. She knew pinning the case on Jax would free her man. All the government had was the word of a bunch of felons. Once they followed through on the plans to implicate Jax, he was done. They just had to make it through the weekend.

· · · ·

"THAT WAS DELICIOUS!" Junior cheered of the fresh lobster dinner. "And now for desert."

He stood and clapped twice, sending people in motion. On cue, a procession of local children appeared bearing flowers. Torches were lit all around and he stood and reached for Marisol's hand.

"What's going on here?" she asked, knowing what ever it was, was for her. She gasped when he produced a stunning 6-karat diamond ring. A traditional preacher was next to appear as Junior explained.

"I want you to marry me. I want us to spend the rest of our lives together," he said as he lowered to one knee. She was too elated for words and almost gave herself a concussion from nodding so hard.

"Oh wow," Megan said with mixed emotions. On one hand it was the most romantic thing she'd ever witnessed or even heard about. On the other, they were supposed to be arresting these guys. Jax was the only one unmoved; he had his own agenda in mind.

"We're next," Jax whispered as the preacher said his piece on their way to pronouncing them man and wife. "Say yes."

"Yes," Megan said as she squinted up at him in wonder. She couldn't believe he just asked her to marry him. Kenneka may have said 'yes' but Megan still wanted to kill him. Still, Detective Robinson planned to put him in prison.

"I now pronounce you man and wife," he proclaimed. Marisol tippy toed up to kiss her handsome husband. He reached around and palmed her ass and stuck his tongue in his mouth.

"Well, I'll see you guys in the morning," Marisol giggled as her husband led her away. He had a honeymoon suite set up on the beach under the moonlight.

"Let's go," Jax said and took her by the hand. Megan ran through a bunch of excuses as he led her back to their bungalow.

'My period, headache, cramps, hair bump' her mind scrambled as he laid her down on the bed. She was still searching when he pulled the thin thong strip away from her vagina. A tear escaped her eye when his tongue flicked across her labia.

"Mm," Jax said as he pulled back to watch her vagina bloom and blossom. Megan surprised herself when her hips lifted to help him remove her thong.

Jax began with long licks like a kid with ice cream. A gush of juice began to leak from her lips in reply.

"Quit playing," she demanded and pulled his face into her crotch. He replied by sticking his tongue deep inside of her. He smiled mentally when he felt how tight she was and squeezed his tongue. They were both relieved when he sucked her to a quit nut but for different reasons.

She was grateful to get off and he was eager to get inside of her. Megan locked eyes with her father's killer as he wriggled his dick between her slippery vaginal lips. She winced in pain and pleasure as he sank down inside of. Soft kisses accompanied the slow, easy strokes and eye contact as they made love.

Jax reached around and gripped handfuls of her fat ass and pushed all the way inside. He took two more strokes and exploded inside of her.

He stuck his tongue back in her mouth and grinded as he filled her with semen. They rested for a moment and repeated the process. Rest and repeat, rest and repeat for the rest of the night.

Chapter 25

Megan felt helpless as she came all over Jax dick the next morning. She pretended he was Floyd as he slid in from behind when they awoke. Once again he pumped her full of cum since she said it was his pussy.

"Shit!" Jax fussed when he felt himself on the verge of another orgasm. His body tensed as he let go.

"Shit is right," Megan purred deceptively. She really meant this was some real bullshit. She was supposed to be putting handcuffs on his wrist, not creamy cum on his dick. "I hate to leave this place."

"We'll be back. We're next to get married on the beach," he assured her. They rolled out of bed and into the shower. Their plane left for the states in an hour, so it was time to go. After another sex bout under the rain head, that is. Megan dressed in a designer dress for the flight home.

"You're glowing!" Marisol cheered when they met up for the ride to the airport.

"Like you?" she shot back with a giggle. They made girly small talk until they were air born and leaned in to talk business.

"Look. I'll give you the keys and the address to the stash spot. They're bringing back a hundred kilos right now. He is turning that over to Jax tomorrow, but not the stash. Wait until we get our cash first tho," she insisted with another giggle.

"How much?" Megan heard herself ask. She knew a hundred kilos was worth millions on the street.

"Just half a mil or so. The change from last week. My husband said I can have it," she gushed and glanced at her ring once more. They made playful banter for the rest of the ride to Atlanta as the men talked business.

"Got some major moves in the works!" Junior nodded and smiled.

"Me, too," Jax nodded along with him. He smiled, too, but without a trace a mirth or merriment.

• • • •

MEGAN AND MARISOL SAID their goodbye with a hug and got in passenger sides of expensive cars. Megan was deep in thought as Jax drove through the city. She both hoped she did and hoped she didn't have to sleep with him again. Her vagina betrayed her as it began to throb when they reached the condo.

"I have to make a run. See you tomorrow?" he asked and walked her to the door.

"Sure, OK," she agreed with a sigh of relief. She would fuck him again if she had too and would enjoy it, but his ass was still going to jail. They shared a long loving kiss in her doorway before he pulled his tongue out and departed. Megan didn't even bother locking the door since she knew Fatimah was on the way. She waited until the footsteps drew near and pulled the door open. "Hello, Miss Fatimah. Yes, I had fun. No ,I did not sleep with him,"

"Mmhm," she hummed as she expected her. She lifted her chin to check for hickies, then sniffed searching for signs of sex. Her head nodded in approval when she passed the test. "So how was Belize?"

"Great!" she cheered and filled her in on how magnificent the country was. It would be the only truth she could tell her only friend.

Meanwhile, Jax drove straight over to Junior's mansion. The security was expecting him and let him in the gate and house with no problem. He took the spiral steps by twos and rushed down the hall. The sounds of sex paused him for a moment at the door before he barged in. Junior had such a good stroke going, he couldn't even stop to talk.

"Jax, what the, fuck... man?" he asked steady pounding. Marisol had her thick legs on his shoulders giving it up completely.

"Coup d'etat," he explained. He expounded further by firing a round into his back, then raised it a few inches for a coup de grace. "Hostile takeover."

"No!" Marisol pleaded when her dead husband slumped on her chest. "I'm a co..."

"A what?" he asked sarcastically and turned his head and lifted a hand his ear. She didn't repeat herself, so he shrugged and turned to leave.

"Damn!" Junior's former head of security said, seeing the murdered couple.

"Yeah," Jax shrugged again. "Clean this shit up. Get rid of this gun. I'm moving my girl in soon."

"You got it, boss man," he said and prepared to follow directions. He nodded at the pretty plastic polymer pistol and decided to keep it. He shrugged and tucked it in his waist.

"Niggas will do anything for a raise," Jax laughed to himself as he walked out. Junior's people had sold him out for a larger slice of the pie. The same way Junior sold out his own dad. His father died in a federal pen and he died in some good, hot Puerto Rican pussy. He still had to divert the drugs from the trip before they reached the stash house. He had his own network set up and was prepared to take flight.

• • • •

"WHO!" MEGAN CALLED as she marched to answer her doorbell the following morning. She peeped out the peephole and saw Jax smiling back. "Fucking bastard... Hey baby! What you doing here!"

"Miss me?" Jax asked and leaned down for a kiss. Megan swallowed her pride and gave him one.

"Of course! Where you been? I called," she pouted. The clock was ticking before she was pulled off the case and he disappeared for two days. Marisol wouldn't answer and her chance to put him away was dwindling by the second. She had set the set up in motion, but needed him to do his part.

"Had business. Get dressed, you're moving," he said and plopped down on her sofa.

"Moving? What about my condo? School? My dad! My furniture!" she said quite believably. Megan had gotten used to the plush life and couldn't see going back to the projects.

"Well, I can replace the furniture and clothes. I would love to meet your dad..."

Megan walked over the love seat and pulled the nine-millimeter from under the cushion. Jax smiled at the gun as she lifted it and aimed it at his face. The first shot knocked the smile clean off his face. The second popped the top of his head off. Megan climbed on the sofa and emptied the entire clip into his face.

"Megan?" Jax asked and snapped her from her daydream. "Yo, you had the craziest look on your face! What was on your mind?"

"Just thinking about my dad. I'm going to tell you about him. Soon, very soon," she assured him and went to pack a bag of panties and toiletries. She packed light since she didn't plan on staying long. Once he took her to where he laid his head she could finish him off. "I just went shopping. Can you take my bags to the new place?"

"Of course," Jax agreed and began carrying the designer clothes and shoe boxes to his car. His trunk was loaded by the time she showered and dressed.

"You're sweating!" she said and wiped his brow with her palm as he walked her out to the Bentley.

"That stuff was heavy!" he laughed and held her door open. Megan spreaded her legs enough to let him see she wasn't wearing panties as she sat down. The plump mound of vagina changed his plans for the day.

• • • •

"HONEY, WE'RE HOME," Jax said when he pulled up to his new home. Megan knew in an instant why Marisol wasn't answering her phone. Dead people never do. For them to be here meant they were both dead. At least they got to spend the rest of their lives together.

"Where are Junior and Marisol?" she asked in near panic. She knew he planned to turn the operations over to Jax and hoped he hadn't murdered them anyway.

"Who?" Jax asked with a curious frown. Marisol's last words haunted him as he tried to figure out what she was saying just before he shot her.

"Safiya, her family calls her Marisol at home. Can you make love to me?" she blurted to distract him from her slip. It did the trick and changed the subject.

"I most certainly can," he assured her and came around to open her door. She treated him to another crotch shot as she stepped out.

"Don't forget my bags," she whined as he began to escort her to the house. "I want to model my new negligee for you,"

"OK," he agreed again and grabbed a few bags. "The rest will have to wait,"

Megan shrugged since what he brought inside was enough. She noticed he completely redecorated Junior's whole house. The same security lounged around the den but the vibe was a lot less formal. Jax took Megan straight up to the bedroom and undressed.

All she had to do was pull the dress over her head and she was just as naked as he was. She climbed on the middle of the bed and got in position with her face down and ass up.

"Lunch is served!" he cheered and clapped. He came in behind her and began to eat her out. He had to hold her in place when it got good to her. She began to wiggle and whine as the first orgasm swept over her.

Jax wasted no time in working his erection inside of her. He grimaced, as he looked down in time to see her coat his dick with her creamy come. He slid a finger in her ass just like he use to do her mother. She came instantly, just like her mother. Just like her mother, she collapsed on her stomach when she came but he stayed with her and pounded out a nut of his own.

"Shit! That's good!" he cheered and rolled off into his own back, panting like a lion after a chase.

"Mmm, yeah it is," Megan agreed. She rolled over and laid on his chest for pillow talk. "I love when you go down on me. I be wanting to do you but..."

"But what?" Jax asked, ready to slay whatever but was keeping him out of her mouth.

"Well first, I never did it before, but I seen a video. It looks fun, but I don't like when the guy grabs her by the head," she said with a frown and headshake.

"I don't do that! I keep my hands by my side!" he assured her. He flattened them to his side as demonstration. "See!"

"Let me cuff you to the bed? Then I'll try it," she said and practiced on his index finger. She twirled her tongue around his fingertip then took it completely into her mouth. He got rock hard again in an instant and instantly agreed. He watched Megan's fat ass jiggle ass she jumped up and rushed to her purse. He had some questions about why she had two pairs of handcuffs in her purse but they would have to wait 'til later. He was about to get his dick sucked now and that took precedence.

"Not too tight," said the one time bad cop who deliberately put cuffs on too tight. A suspect would tell anything he knew to get them from cutting into his skin.

"K," she said and secured his first wrist. He frowned at her academy perfect technique but got distracted by her breast in his face when she reached over to cuff the other wrist. He sucked her nipple as she clicked the cuff in place. She let him suck her nipple until he stopped on his own since it felt so good.

"Where you going? What are you doing?" he asked when she got off the bed and began to get dressed.

"You're the one who's going somewhere," she laughed dryly. She pulled her phone and made a call. "Detective Sergeant Robinson, requesting back up at..."

"What the fuck!" Jax said hearing her call in their exact address. He recognized the authentic cop codes that sent the task force and all available local cops in their direction. He couldn't help but laugh at the good try. "Nice try, but what do I have? Nothing. No dope, no money, no nothing,"

"Well, those shoe boxes full of cocaine say otherwise," she laughed and pointed at the bags he carried in for her. "Plus, the rest you left in your car,"

"You little bitch!" he barked and tugged at the cuffs. The headboard creaked but didn't budge. Megan got a good laugh at his predicament.

"Actually, I was going to kill you. Just like you did my father. You remember my father, don't you? Your partner, Detective Robinson?" she asked feeling her blood begin to boil. The sirens in the distance were the only things that prevented her from fulfilling her vision and shooting him in his face.

"Yeah, I remember him. And I'm going to kill you just like I did him," he laughed. His mocking laughter grew louder and louder until Megan couldn't take it anymore. She rushed over and shoved the gun in his mouth so hard it chipped his tooth. He gagged when it touched his tonsils and her finger tightened on the trigger.

"Police! Search warrant!" the police shouted as they breached the house. They spreaded out and secured the house and occupants until they reached the bedroom.

"Don't do it, Robinson," Agent Hernandez pleaded softly from behind her. "Don't go to jail for him,"

"I'm not. I'm a good cop, just like my father. You cost him his life but you won't cost me mine," she growled and removed her gun from his larynx. "They gonna put you under the jail this time!"

Chapter 26

"The bodies of an unidentified man and woman were found in a wooded area north of Atlanta. It's probably that of Junior Rodriguez and Marisol Ruiz," Hernandez said as he debriefed the squad. Megan knocked the lone tear from her face and lifted her chin when her name was mentioned. "Thanks to Detective Robinson, Jax was caught with enough drugs to put him away for the rest of his life."

Megan stopped paying attention and drifted inside of her head. She made her case and got her man, but was it at the expense of her own soul. She got her man but gave up more than she had to give. For the first time in her life, she didn't want to be a cop any more. Especially a bad cop.

Not only did she plant all the drugs found in the house, but she also kept the money she found in the stash house. It was wrong, but she deserved it. It would jump start her new life because she wasn't going back to her old one. A smile spread on her face as a plan came to mind. Once the briefing was done, she approached the boss to pitch her idea.

"I need you to identify Marisol's body as me. I don't need any of Junior's crew coming after me," she explained.

"Hmp? That's not a bad idea?" he nodded and rubbed his chin.

"It's a great idea," she corrected. "I can't do this anymore. Let me rest in peace." The agent agreed and extended his hand to shake. Megan looked up into his eyes and handed him her badge instead. She turned and walked away and never looked back.

• • • •

"SO, YOU'RE A COP?" Fatimah dared and twisted her lips dubiously.

"I was. I'm retired now. My real name is Megan. Megan Robinson. Everything else is a lie except our friendship," she explained. There was a brief silence save the news playing on the TV. Fatimah still wasn't sure what to believe until breaking news stole the show.

"The bodies of a man and woman found last week have been identified as that of reputed drug dealer, Junior Rodriguez, and undercover officer, Megan Robinson..."

"Told you. Now that I'm dead, I can finally go live" Megan announced and stood to leave

"So, what now?" Fatimah asked with concern in her voice.

"I'm going to back New York and getting married. I hope..." she said and hugged her friend. "Oh, but I need a favor."

"What are you up to?" her friend asked and laughed at the devious look on her face.

"I'm going to a funeral. Mine," she laughed. As bad as Megan wanted to run home to New York to her grandmother and Floyd, she was stuck in Atlanta until Jax was indicted in a month. That gave her the chance to attend her own funeral.

"Can't see a thing," Megan grumbled as she walked into their church wearing one of Fatimah's over garments and veil. She shook her head vainly at the academy picture they chose to stand beside her closed casket. Her head constantly shook at the phony display of grief by the cops who knew the box was empty. The preacher preached about her death as if he actually knew her in life. The service wrapped up and she headed back to her hotel to wait for the court date.

Megan and Floyd spent most nights on the phone and got reacquainted. His girlfriend got the hint and got ghost after a week. Both planned to ask the other to marry the other when she returned to New York.

• • • •

FINALLY, MEGAN GUSHED when the alarm awoke her on Jax's court day. The hearing started at 9 and her flight left at noon. Tonight she would be having dinner with her beloved grandmother and brother and Pretty Boy Floyd would be desert.

Dinner was a long way off, so she stopped by the breakfast bar to quiet her grumbling stomach. She couldn't wait to see the look on Jax's face when she took the stand to testify. He knew she faked her death not to have problems with Junior's people, so he put the blame for his death on his security team. It would be easy since one was caught with tin murder weapon. Without her to say otherwise he, was Scott free again.

"Cant wait to get me some bagels," she moaned at the grits, bacon and other country cooking. The smell of the fried pork wafted up into her nostrils and made her gag. She tried to fight the nausea, but it got the best of her and sent her rushing into the bathroom to throw up. She suddenly recognized the strange symptoms she'd been having the last few days. She experienced them years before when she got pregnant the first time. Only this time she had no doubt who the father was.

. . . .

HOW DOES THE DEFENDANT plead to the charges of murder, possession with intent to distribute... " the judge asked as he read a grocery list of charges. Jax stood there with a cocky smirk on his face knowing they didn't have much without Megan.

All heads including his turned when a late comer to the proceedings came in and took a seat. All eyes seen her, but Jax looked like he saw a ghost.

I thought she was supposed to be dead! Jax moaned loud enough to disturb the judge. He knew she was alive somewhere, but didn't expect her to be resurrected at his hearing.

"No, but you are," she snickered loud enough for Jax to hear. She knew her testimony would get him the death penalty and that was the next best thing to killing him herself. Either way he would no longer be breathing and that was cool with her.

"Can I have a word with my client?" his attorney asked as their smug smirks got turned upside down. The judge acquiesced with a nod and they huddled up like it was fourth and one with two seconds to go. His attorney advised him to take a plea or take a lethal injection. Jax let out a sigh that could be heard throughout the courtroom. He shook his head and whispered back with his own idea. They negotiated back and forth like a used car deal and decided on a price.

His attorney stepped over and pitched his idea to the prosecutor. He too nodded in agreement and the deal and turned um the judge.

"Your honor, the state is willing to drop the murder charges against the defendant in exchange for ten years and his testimony against the Rodriquez crime family," he said while Jax lowered his head in defeat.

"Hell naw!" someone shouted before the judge got a chance tp answer. Megan realized it was she who made the outburst when all eyes turned in her direction. She slowly sank back in her seat and pouted. She was powerless to intervene as he got another sweetheart of a deal. She, too, accepted defeat and slunk from the courtroom when Jax got a mere slap on the wrist.

• • • •

"I KNOW I BETTER NOT be!" Megan demanded as she peed on a test strip in the airport bathroom. She put it aside and peed on two more. Her flight number was announced to board, so she tucked them into her purse and rushed out.

Megan's mind flashed to all the designer clothes and purses she got to keep from her undercover work. Her supervisor just shrugged and told her to keep it when she tried to turn them in. They didn't know anything about the money though. She planned on putting it to good use. Sleep crept up on her while she planned.

"Ma'am?" a flight attendant asked as she touched Megan's arm.

"What!" she shouted and jumped to her feet to fight. She felt silly when she looked around the deserted plane. Panic gripped her as she remembered her bag in the overhead bin. The half a million in cash would have been like hitting the lottery for whoever walked off with it. She let out a sigh of relief when it was still there. She nodded an apology to the woman and got off the plane.

"There she is!" Jax shouted and pointed, while hopping up and down when he spotted his sister. He was a smooth operator around the way but was still Megan's little brother. He took off and hopped the security gate to get to her.

• • • •

"HE'S COOL," FLOYD SAID, showing his badge. Megan would have shown hers as well except she turned it in when she resigned. Instead she threw her arms open and braced herself for impact.

"Ugh!" Megan grunted when he slammed into her, sending them both scrambling on the ground. "I see you missed me, huh, Jax?"

"No, I... wait, you called me Jax!" he shouted excitedly. "You called me Jax!"

"That's your name, ain't it, crazy boy!" she said, shaking her head.

"Well, they call me Juelz now, so..." he explained. Dianne smiled broadly at her grandkids loving each other. She was next to get a hug and kiss from Megan.

"Hello grandmother," she said and squeezed the frail old lady. She was done with project life, but planned to take her with her wherever she went. Her grandmother released her as Floyd stepped up.

"Hey," Megan greeted shyly to Floyd. She viewed him in a new light now that she realized she wanted to be with him.

"Hey, yourself," he replied with a wide smile. They would save their hugs and kisses until they were alone later. That was private, but Floyd had a public question to pop.

"Hey now!" Dianne squealed when Floyd began to take a knee. The national anthem wasn't playing so it could only be one thing.

"Megan Robinson, will you do me the honor of becoming my wife?" he appealed and produced a one karat solitaire. It was nowhere as big as the one Junior gave Marisol but then again, he wasn't a multimillionaire drug dealer either. He was a cop and the ring set him back three months salary.

Megan suddenly remembered the pregnancy test in her purse. A tear escaped her eye wondering what the results were.

"Don't be no punk!" her brother cheered from the sideline when she knocked the tear away.

"Answer the man!" Dianne fussed like a grandmother. Megan's head began to nod slowly as she agreed to be his wife.

"Yes," she croaked with guilt and sorry in her throat. Floyd heard it, too, and knew they would talk about it when they got to his apartment later that night.

• • • •

THE FAMILY HAD AN ANIMATED dinner on City Island to welcome Megan home. Floyd drove them back to the projects to drop Dianne and Jax off before taking Megan home. She had been talking some cash shit on the phone over the last month and now it was time to pay up. Megan rushed straight into his bathroom as soon as they went inside.

"Oh man!" Megan groaned when she finally looked at the test strips. All the said the same thing and made her knees buckle.

"You OK in there?" Floyd called when he heard her outburst in his bathroom.

"No," she whined as she came back out. She couldn't find words to explain, so she handed him the test strips. His face twisted into a question mark, marked by pain.

"So, but...," he asked in confusion. "I thought we, I mean, we're supposed to get married?"

"I was undercover. I did what I had to do to make my case," she said and cringed at how disgusting it sounded. She felt filthy and unworthy of being a wife. She sighed and stood to leave. "I'm sorry, I..."

"Wait," he said and took her hand. He sat her back down but neither had any words to say. They sat there in silence for hours until he took her to bed. The telephone promises of what they would do to each other would have to wait for some other time. Instead they snuggled up and drifted off to sleep.

She wasn't sure if this was the end of their relationship, but it is the end of the story.

The end

Epilogue

OK, so I know I vowed to never have another abortion, but fuck that! No way was I having a child by my mama's baby daddy, brother's father and my father's killer. Fuck that. Floyd drove me to the clinic and made them get me in the next day. We got married at city hall a week after that. He had to wait to get some, but so did I. So we were even. Still I was pregnant again in a couple of months.

I had to come clean about the money, but Floyd wasn't mad. He quit the force, too, and we both enrolled in college. He's going to be a lawyer and I decided to follow my friend Fatimah's lead and enrolled as a pre med student. I used a hundred thousand dollars to renovate the house on Long Island after the damage my mom and Reese did. Of course I brought my brother and grandmother along with me.

I couldn't forget about Jax though. No way was he getting off so easy again. I had to spend fifty thousand to make sure he got what he had coming...

• • • •

"PHONE CALL, JAX," PABLO said as he peeked in his cell. Jax put his book down and let him into his cell and took the outstretched cell phone.

It's like that?" Jax said as three more Latinos rushed in behind him. He expected them to try him one day for testifying against the family. It looked like today was that day.

"Just like that," Pablo nodded with an evil grin as the four shanks came out.

"Yeah," Jax said defiantly into the phone. He knew whoever spent the money to send him bye bye wanted to say goodbye. He was shocked to see Megan's fat face on the screen. She was eight months pregnant, but still didn't want to miss this.

"Sup, yo, This is Megan. Just wanted to watch you get murdered," she sang nonchalantly. She got her wish when the men moved in and stabbed him to death and beyond. Now it was really the end.